W9-BVT-957

On The
Stranger's Mountain

On The Stranger's Mountain
by Gladys Baker Bond

Illustrated by Derek Lucas

Abelard-Schuman

London/New York/Toronto

Books by Gladys Baker Bond:

A HEAD ON HER SHOULDERS
THE MYSTERY AT FAR REACH (with Florence Baker Bertram)
ON THE STRANGER'S MOUNTAIN
THE SECRET AT ROCKY RIDGE (with Florence Baker Bertram)

© copyright 1969 by Gladys Baker Bond
Library of Congress Catalogue Card Number: 69:14244
Standard Book Number: 200.71585.2

London	*New York*	*Toronto*
Abelard-Schuman	Abelard-Schuman	Abelard-Schuman
Limited	Limited	Canada Limited
8 King St. WC2	6 West 57th St.	1680 Midland Ave.

Printed in the United States of America

JF
B7113σ

To

NICHOLAS PETER, MY SON

100191

Contents

1

Tick of the Big Watch

A silent group of people left the churchyard. At the head of the rain-drenched line, Otto Meyer walked with Pastor Schmidt. Pastor's black robe collected mud with each step he took. He carried a big Bible against his chest. When Otto looked at him, the man's face softened. Once Pastor touched Mama's elbow. Mama did not seem to notice. Otto wondered if Mama could see through the ugly black veil she wore.

Stumbling through the rain, sometimes stepping on Mama's long black skirt or bumping into each other, came the rest of the Meyer children: Martin, Augustus, Hans and Katherine. Ten-year-old Katherine did not reach for a comforting hand. With shoulders square and chin in the air, she marched alone.

Friends and neighbors reached the gate. They spoke softly to each other and to Mama, then hurried away. Otto mumbled when they spoke to him. He watched them go: the hunchbacked little tailor, Israel Fishbein; Vito Rubino, the grocer; Big Mike, who owned the butcher shop; a couple

9

of the policemen who tried to keep order in Pittsburgh's slum area; Tom-the-printer, and the wispy librarian with the whispering voice who had guided Papa's reading. These were the friends Papa had made in his twelve years in the United States of America. They walked and talked. Papa did not.

Carrying his lunch pail, Papa had left home three days ago. His friends came home that night. In the crowded, drafty shacks perched on hillsides and riverbanks, hungry men ate "payday" supper.

Mama cooked sauerkraut, weiners, and hot fruit dumplings, but Papa did not come home.

A policeman came, then Papa's boss, and the men he worked with in the coal mine. They came to talk to Mama. They brought Papa's lunch pail, his worn purse, and the big watch he had owned in Germany. They talked. Mama stared at the floor. She did not touch the things that had belonged to Papa.

"Put it in your pocket," she told Otto, when he accepted the watch from Papa's boss. "The man of the family carries the watch."

Not yet twelve and "man of the family," Otto now picked up his feet and put them down. Carefully he avoided mudholes, all the way from the churchyard to the house Papa had rented from Big Mike. Otto did not speak. Katherine did not speak, nor did Mama, Martin, Gussie or Hans.

At her own gate Mama shook hands with Pastor. She walked up the cinder path and climbed the many steps.

She crossed the narrow porch, opened the door and went into the house. The children followed.

They stood in a solemn row. They waited for Mama to tell them what to do and how to act in a house without a father.

Mama took off the long black veil. When she hung it on the back of a wooden chair, the veil touched the bare floor. She clasped her hands in her lap and nodded her head, all neatly wrapped around with smooth, blond braids.

She said, "Sit."

Martin, Gussie and Katherine sat in a row on the edge of the cot that served as a couch by day and Otto's bed at night. Katherine held Hans in her lap. She tried to take his thumb from his mouth. She gave up and faced Mama.

Otto could hear the little popping sounds Hans made, sucking his thumb, and the steady ticktick of the big watch in his pocket. It still rained, and the roof was tin. Listening to the rain, Otto thought, "We're living inside a drum."

He wanted to say the words aloud to make Katherine smile. Then he blushed. It did not seem respectful to think cheerful thoughts when he had just come from the churchyard. If he thought of Papa under the lopsided wreath Katherine had made, he would cry. The man in the family must not cry, so Otto thought about the inside of a drum. After a while it was not a cheerful thought. The sping-spingspang of the raindrops hurt his ears and his heart.

Mama broke the long silence. She said firmly, "Otto, bring paper and pencil. We'll write a letter." Mama spoke in German. Inside Otto's German-American head the words

12

became, "A letter to write we shall." Mama spoke no English. The Meyer children had learned to think and speak in two languages.

Otto brought his school tablet and pencil from the high shelf above the cot.

"Otto, sit," Mama said. "Make yourself comfortable. This will be a long letter and very important."

Hans whimpered. Katherine said, "Ssh," then bent to help Gussie untie his tight shoes.

Otto sat at the table in the middle of the room. He wrote the town and state, "Pittsburgh, Pennsylvania," and the date, "May 14, 1921." Then he waited for Mama to name Grandfather Ziegler, Uncle Ernst, Great-uncle Ottmar, or even Aunt Berta Grimm. He hoped he could spell the German words so they could be read by relatives in Hamm and Insterburg. They had not wanted Mama to come to America with Papa. Otto did not want to shame Papa's memory by misspelling the words they would read.

Mama's face grew very red. Tears ran down her cheeks and dripped on her clenched hands. She twisted her wide gold wedding band around and around. Shaking her head to make the tears stop, she said in a small voice, "To Bela Karl Czek, Dear Sir:"

"W-who?" Otto blurted in surprise.

"C-z-e-k," Mama spelled slowly. "It is pronounced Check. Now listen carefully and write what I say."

Very simply Mama told of the accident in the coal mine and of Papa who had not come home, of five fatherless children and of the lack of money.

Mama sat motionless for a long time. The watch ticked in Otto's pocket and Hans sucked his thumb. Gussie took off his shoes. Martin drummed his heels. Katherine flinched when rain rattled the rickety frame of the crowded three-room shack.

Then Mama whispered, "Otto, you will write, 'Mr. Bela Czek, please come. My children and I need you.'"

"N-need?"

Appalled, Otto dropped his pencil. He looked at Mama, who could not have said those shocking words to a man he did not know. Dizzily he stood up and held the table for support. "Who is this man, Mama? Why do you write to him?"

Gently Mama said, "Otto, with all my heart I loved your papa. It is my duty to obey Johann. This is as Johann planned. Johann said, 'When I am gone, you will marry Bela Czek, Anna.' So," Mama finished shakily, "Johann is gone. I will marry Mr. Czek. I have no choice. My children must eat."

Otto turned away, crying soundlessly. Losing Papa had been black trouble, but to lose Mama while she still lived was unbearable.

Mama and Papa had been the two halves of a whole. Who was this Mr. Check? How old was he? What was he like? Was he kind, or stern and Old Country in his habits and thinking? And——"Why, Mama, why?" Otto cried.

Otto did not doubt the love that had bound Johann and Anna Meyer. He had seen it in their eyes. He had heard it in their voices. He had felt it in their touch. There was

14

even love in Papa's grumbling and Mama's scolding. Did love evaporate like dew in the sun when Pastor said some words, prayed a blessing, and marked a cross on air? Otto could not believe it, since his own heart was so filled with loving and remembering.

Then he thought, "Mama is sick. She does not know what she is saying." Thinking so made it possible for him to pick up the pencil. Thinking so could *not* make him write. The pencil felt heavy and long——much too heavy and long.

"Write, Otto," Mama directed. "Mr. Czek will come. He will take care of us as he promised Papa."

"Oh," Otto said stonily. "So he promised Papa. Who is this—this—Mr. Check?"

Otto saw that Katherine listened, wide-eyed and scared. Eight-year-old Martin looked puzzled. Gussie and Hans were too young to understand the words Mama said. Gussie was in first grade, and Hans did not go to school.

Mama said, "At home in Hamm, Bela Czek was Johann's best friend." At that moment she almost smiled, remembering the great friendship of Johann Meyer and Bela Czek. She explained, "We three came to the United States of America together. We were young. The men found work here in Pittsburgh. Bela and Johann went to a class to learn to speak English. Johann talked for me. Bela said I should go to class. Johann said, 'No. Anna belongs in my house.'

"One day Johann hurt his foot. He could not walk. Bela Czek was on night shift. He did not come to our house. I could not ask for help, since I spoke no English. We were cold and hungry.

15

"When Johann could walk again he brought Bela Czek to our house. He said to Bela, 'Mining is dangerous work. If I should die, what would happen to Anna? She does not speak English.'

"Bela said, 'I would marry her. I would take care of Anna.'

"Then Johann said, 'If she has children, will you marry her?'

"And Bela said, 'If she has a dozen children, I will marry her. Don't worry, my good friend Johann. I will take care of Anna.' "

Mama's voice had been flooded with tears while she talked. But she finished in her normal voice. "Johann and Bela Czek shook hands, binding the vow as men do. Then both shook hands with me. We laughed together. Soon after that Bela Czek went to some place called Denver to dig gold. We did not see him again, Johann and I, but now the time has come when I must remind Mr. Czek of his promise to Johann."

Otto could not write the words.

He argued with Mama. He told her, "This is not the American way! You do not marry someone you call 'Mister.' You do not write to him on funeral day!"

Mama wrinkled her blond brows in bewilderment. "Why not? This is when I need him. And who is American? I am German. Mr. Czek is Hungarian. We understand about duty."

"I am American!" Otto cried. "And I do *not* understand this kind of duty." He tapped the table, rap-a-tap, rap-a-tap, till he could not hear the tick of Papa's watch, but he could hear the rain on the tin roof. It changed the house into a drum with echoing words, "Marry, duty, marry, duty." Otto put his hands over his ears; he still heard the words.

Then there was another sound. Mama said, "Johann," with so much stored-up love and sorrow and loneliness, that Otto put down his pencil and walked across the room. He stood by Mama's chair and patted her shaking shoulders.

"I'll take care of you, Mama," he promised. "You don't need Mr. Check. I am the man of the family now."

Mama reached up to pat Otto's hand. Then she said, "Tomorrow we will finish the letter, Otto."

2

The Letter

When morning came, Otto wrote the letter, but he wrote it in English, knowing Mama could not read it. He left out the part about marriage. As the man of the family, Otto could not allow Mama to remind Mr. Bela Czek of his promise to marry her. Otto agreed that Papa's oldest friend should be told about the accident, but that is all he would say.

While Otto wrote, Katherine hovered about the table. She was supposed to be washing dishes. She spent more time peering over Otto's shoulder than she spent at the dishpan.

"Trinka, you're bothering me," Otto muttered. With the eraser of his pencil he scrubbed out a word. He bore down on the lead to correct his spelling.

Earnestly Katherine begged, "I just want to know what you are writing to that man. She's *my* mother, too!"

Otto watched Katherine's lips tremble, then stiffen in a smile-shape when Mama came into the room. Otto creased the sheet of rough, ruled paper. Before he could put the letter into its envelope, Katherine took the paper out of his hands.

"I want to see if the words are spelled right," Katherine told Mama. Her eyes dared Otto to object.

Otto said nothing. He knew Mama would see no wrong in Katherine's reading the letter. His sister was especially good in reading and spelling. Papa had been proud of the report cards she brought home.

Anxiously, Mama puckered her blond brows and asked, "Is it a good letter, Katrinka?"

Katherine read slowly. She looked straight into Otto's eyes, sharing his secret and approving. "Oh yes, Mama," she said. "It is a good letter."

Mama, too, scanned the letter. She scolded, "But why did you not write it in German? How will Johann's friend, Mr. Czek, read the English words?"

Otto dropped his lashes so Mama would not be able to read the guilt in his eyes. He told her, "Probably Papa's friend writes English by this time. After all, you said he has been speaking it for twelve years. If he doesn't read, he can ask somebody to read his letter to him."

Carefully Otto addressed the envelope, "Mr. Bela Karl Czek, Denver, Colorado." He put on the stamp, walked down the steep road to the corner and put the letter in the mailbox. Then he shoved his hands in his pockets and muttered, "I hope you have moved a long way off——to Alaska, maybe, Mr. Bela Karl Check. *I'm* the man in this family now."

Sturdily Otto squared his shoulders. When he glimpsed himself in a dirty window, he wished those shoulders to be wider and balanced on the end of a longer spine. How was

19

he to earn money to take care of Mama and Katrinka, Martin, Gussie and Hans?

Not yet twelve years old, Otto had three weeks more to spend in grade school before promotion to junior high school. Also, he was small for his age; small and dark enough to have been the son of Vito Rubino. The rest of the Meyer children were blue-eyed towheads. One day Gussie would be as big as Papa, maybe bigger. Trinka, the only girl, would be pretty like Mama.

Otto, the firstborn, was short, thin, quick-moving and monkeyfaced. He thought about his shortcomings all the way home. By the time he reached the gate, Otto almost regretted having changed Mama's letter to Papa's friend.

Then he felt the bulge of Papa's big watch in his pocket and heard its steady ticking. Feeling the start of tears, he thought, "All I can do is try, Papa. Just try."

When Otto went into the house he found Mama, his sister, and three brothers at the table. They were not eating. They were watching Mama count the money that had been in Papa's purse. The accident had happened the day the men were paid. Though Papa had collected his wages, he had not been able to spend one cent. It was all there on the table in front of Mama, neatly separated in little stacks of dollars, halves, quarters, dimes, nickels and pennies. There were more pennies than dollars.

"Otto?" Mama called when the door opened. "How long before Mr. Czek will get his letter? Do we have money enough to last till he comes?"

Otto looked at the money. He looked at Mama. When his eyes blurred, he ran from the house.

20

The Letter

After a while Otto wandered down to the river. Some boys from his class were fishing from the bank below the railroad tracks. One of them said, "Tough luck, Ott, losing your old man." The rest stared, then picked up cans of mud and fishworms. They found new fishing holes.

Otto watched barges plow past, burdened with iron ore, limestone, coal and coke needed to make Pittsburgh's steel. Ore cars rolled on the rails lining the river's edge. Fog moved close to the water. Above the fog hung a thick layer of steel mill smoke. Around Otto rose the hills, cluttered with ugliness and wrapped in a mist of fog and smoke.

He thought, "Somewhere, outside the city, maybe, life must be different, not so confused." But here was smoke, a dirty river, crowding barges and shabby houses on rocky land. Here lived an anthill of people who were no longer German, not Italian, not Polish or Russian or Welsh—and certainly not American.

"What are we?" Otto cried inside himself. "Without Papa, what will happen to us?"

His stomach ached when he thought of Mama's stern red face and her shocking decision to marry a man who would feed her children.

He watched dirty water grumble around a rusted milk can and some old packing cases. A leather boot half-filled with mud caught some of the water, but mostly the water just ran. On and on and on, the water ran.

Papa said this water was used many times to cool the steel before it ever reached the water pipes that supplied the city. "Is it good that we should drink this water?" Mama had asked. Papa shrugged. His voice sounded prideful when he said, "That smoke and that much-used water is our bread and butter. Steel! That is the important thing. Steel! For that I dig the coal."

"I can't dig coal or make steel," Otto thought bleakly. "I'm not big enough, not old enough, not strong enough." Mama's way could *not* be the right way, but what could Otto offer to replace her plan?

He could not ask for welfare. Papa would turn over in his grave. "We earn our bread," was Papa's unbreakable code.

Otto picked up some chunks of coal that had rattled from ore cars. Listlessly he threw coal at a telephone pole. Then he hunched his shoulders and wandered through a litter of rusty cans, soggy paper boxes, socks with holes and shoes without mates. At last he reached the back doors of the shabby stores that leaned against each other on a street sliced out of rock.

Otto looked at the river. The fog was lifting. Up here a thin spring sun warmed the hillside. He hoped the sun warmed the churchyard, too.

Vito Rubino sat near the back door of his grocery store. On Vito's right lay a great mound of shriveled potatoes and a heap of limp gunnysacks; on his left, a stack of moderately clean bushel baskets. The little Italian rubbed pale, long sprouts from the potatoes. He threw away the rotten vegetables and tossed the rest into one of the baskets.

After a while, Otto sat down beside Vito and began to break off sprouts.

"Feelsa good, sitting in the sun," Vito said cheerfully.

Otto nodded.

22

"Feelsa good, busy with the hands."

Again Otto nodded.

"You no talk, I no talk," Vito said. "Okay?"

Side by side, man and boy, they worked. Sprouts dropped. Potatoes fell into place, now here, now there. At last Vito said, "Looka here, keed. You want I should give you some of these potatoes? Helpa yourself! Take home to your mama alla vegetables you can carry!"

"You mean it, Mr. Rubino?" Otto asked.

"Sure, I mean it. You helpa me, I helpa you."

Otto's hands flew.

When the bell clanged, Vito went into the store to wait on a customer. He did not come back for almost an hour. By the time Vito was free, only a dozen potatoes remained to clean and sort.

"Gooda work, gooda work, keed!" Vito said. He snatched up one of the gunnysacks and thrust it into Otto's hands. "You holda, I filla da bag." Vito scooped up potatoes while he talked.

As the bag filled, Otto warned, "Don't give me more than I earned. I don't want charity."

"Who talks abouta charity?" Vito asked, flinging out both hands. "You work. I pay. Thatsa all."

Before he closed the sack, the talkative Italian tossed in a bunch of garlic buds, some onions and a huge red cabbage. "Now, eat!" he said, grinning widely.

Otto hunched under his sack like a miniature Kris Kringle. He took a few steps, then turned back to look at the discard pile. He said, "Mama could cut away the bad spots."

Vito started to object, then stopped himself. His large black eyes softened with understanding. Softly he said, "Okay, keed, okay. You wanta da potatoes, you bringa sack. Helpa yourself."

Gladly Otto hobbled around the store and into the street. When he reached the butcher shop, Big Mike leaned in the doorway. His fat hands patted a soiled canvas apron. Big Mike hailed Otto. "Hey, Ott! You want a bone for your dog?"

"You know we don't have a dog, Mike," Otto said soberly.

"Then take a bone for the dog you don't have," Mike said. He went into the shop. He came back with a lumpy package wrapped in pinkish brown paper. Otto added the bones to the treasures in his gunnysack. Before he picked up the sack he told Big Mike, "I'll be back to sweep your floor or wash your window. I work for my family's food."

Big Mike clapped a ham-sized hand on Otto's thin shoulder. He bellowed, "You'll make out, Ott."

Up the steep, soot-grimed street Otto hobbled, filled to bursting with pride. He had worked. Tonight his family would eat. Not Papa's labor, but his, would fill their plates.

When Otto thumped his heavy gunnysack to the porch floor, Mama flew to open the door. Otto saw that she had been crying. When she saw the vegetables and meat, she gasped out her wonder at this, her so generous, so wonderful son.

Otto blushed with pleasure. He swaggered just a bit. He marshaled Martin, Katherine and even Gussie to help carry home the unsalable potatoes.

"I will help," Mama offered. "Gussie is so small."

"No," Otto said. "Papa says—said—woman's place is in the home."

"Ach, your father," Mama choked.

That night Mama sat up late, peeling, cutting and cooking the potatoes Vito had thrown away. The children went to bed well-stuffed with potato cakes. Otto opened his arithmetic book to work on the lesson Papa's accident had interrupted.

He could not keep his mind on multiplication and division. The house was filled with the odor of boiling meat, for the bone Big Mike had given was generously fleshed with good, red beef. When Mama lifted the pot lid, Otto heard a soft little hum of song.

Otto bent over his tablet. Tomorrow he must return to school, but after school he must find another job. He had a family to feed, and that letter on its way to Colorado did not mention a duty marriage.

3

How Old Are You, Mama?

On Monday morning Otto listened for the first creak of bedsprings to tell him Mama had awakened. He built the fire in the range and carried the wash-boiler from the porch. He put the boiler on the back of the stove, then filled it with water to heat for Mama's washing. On the back porch he set two tubs side by side on the heavy wash-bench. One tub he filled with cold water for Mama's rinsing. The other he half-filled, ready for the last-minute addition of boiling water and melted lye soap. He was scrubbing soot-grime from the wire clotheslines when Mama stepped onto the narrow porch.

It pleased Otto that Mama had rested well. Blue shadows lay at the top of her cheekbones, but there were no fresh tearstains. Her step was brisk. When a robin somersaulted in pulling up its worm from the packed earth, she chuckled.

Otto smiled, too, glad to share this small delight. He watched Mama's hands tie her apron. He thought, "Why, Mama is young. I didn't know . . ."

That meant Papa had been young, too. Otto had never thought about the number of their years. Mama was Mama and Papa was Papa and they were just there, the solid background of his life.

"How old are you, Mama?" he asked suddenly.

Mama widened her blue eyes, surprised that he asked. "Old? I am twenty-eight. You know that."

Wonderingly, Otto said, "Then I am almost half your age, Mama."

"I was sixteen when you were born," Mama said.

"And Papa?" Otto asked.

"Papa was nineteen," Mama said proudly. "So strong, so handsome, Johann."

Nineteen, with a wife and baby son to support; why, Papa had been a boy when he crossed that ocean and shook hands with a man named Bela Karl Czek.

Boys often made promises. While they stood close and touched palms they meant every word they said, no matter how wild the promise. Did that promise hold for a lifetime? Otto thought not. He himself had promised to run away to Alaska with a boy whose name he did not know. They had met on a hot day. It had seemed such an excellent idea, so reasonable a thing to do. "But I didn't go," Otto reasoned.

Otto bunched his cleaning rag into a hard wad. He asked the question that had been on his mind. "How old was—was Mr. Check?"

"He was older than my Johann, I think." The throaty German words rolled out and silky blond lashes fluttered while Mama thought. "Twenty-five, maybe. Yes, I'm sure. He was twenty-five."

A boy and a young man, Otto thought. Big boys, not men, had shaken hands and parted. Since Papa was

28

nineteen twelve years ago, he had died at thirty-one. This Bela Check would be less than forty years of age, thirty-seven, probably. A lot could have happened in twelve years. The man might have married. By this time he could be the father of a large family, happily married, with the handshaking and the promises long forgotten. "That's it," Otto decided. "That's the way it has to be."

While Otto finished cleaning the clotheslines on the steep hillside, he watched smoke from stovepipes join smoke in the sky. He thought about the men in those houses. In this neighborhood men married young, fathered large families and lived in the Old Country way. German, Italian, Welsh, Irish and Swedish. customs mixed into a kind of stew, till who knew or could separate the one from the other? They were all held together by a kind of gravy of hardship and struggle.

A few men, like Papa, dreamed big. They sent their boys to high school, as Papa had planned to send his sons. At twelve, those sons thought about baseball, not potatoes.

The unmarried young men hung around the riverfront. They yelled themselves hoarse at prizefights. They shouted and fought, ate popcorn and hot dogs, and danced with their girls on Saturday night. On Monday night everybody went into the city——miners, millworkers, sweethearts. Those young men did not look at or think about widows with five children, one of them soon to be a man.

Well, Otto thought. That takes care of Mr. Bela Check! He won't even remember Mama. "I hope," Otto muttered.

Otto followed Mama into the crowded kitchen. She fried a great mound of potatoes. Katherine poured mugs of coffee. For the younger children the coffee was sugared and weakened with canned milk. Otto and Katherine drank their coffee black, and Martin received only a spoonful of milk in his coffee mug.

While the children ate, Mama sliced buns. These she spread with peanut butter and wrapped in napkins. She handed the packages to Katherine, Martin and Gussie. Otto held out his hand, but Mama sat down to eat her breakfast.

Otto craned his neck to see if his sandwich remained on the breadboard. "My sandwich, Mama," he reminded.

"Why?" Mama asked.

"For school," Otto said.

"Oh." Mama chewed and swallowed. Then she said, "No."

"No, what?" Otto asked uneasily. He did not like the direction of this conversation.

Katherine, Martin and Gussie stopped chewing to listen. They did not smile.

"No more school," Mama said. "You are the firstborn. Until Mr. Czek comes to keep his promise, you must find a job and work."

"Mama!" Otto cried. "This is not the Old Country! This is America. I *must* go to school. If I don't go, the truant officer will pick me up."

"Why?" Mama asked.

"It is the law, Mama, that I must go to school," Otto said.

Mama shook her blond head. "I do not understand this law that says a son may not help his mother."

Loudly Otto said, "And I don't understand the Old

Country with its handshaking and duties and no school."
Otto was so shaken by the unexpected scene with Mama
that he answered her in English. Then he ran from the
house without a sandwich.

Feet clattered on the crackled walk. Before he reached
the corner, Katherine caught up with Otto. She panted,
"Y-you forgot your books, and your t-tablet, and I b-brought
them."

"Thanks, Trinka," Otto said stiffly.

"I'll give you my sandwich," Katherine offered.

"Aw . . ." Otto began an objection.

"I ate lots of potatoes," Katherine explained. "I won't
be hungry. You got up early and worked and didn't finish
your breakfast."

Silently the bereaved children walked toward school. A
block behind them Martin and Gussie walked together.
Otto could hear the solemn dong-dong of the big school
bell.

Smoke boiled into the sky. It rose from dozens of
foundries; iron and steel works, furnaces, machine shops,
and factories where men made steam boilers and engines
and nails. Otto thought of the copper smelters and rolling
mills, the oil refineries, the white lead and glass works,
cotton mills, canneries and all the other factories that
elbowed for room.

He thought of the steamboats carrying goods throughout
the Mississippi valley and of the railways and canals that
joined Pittsburgh with Philadelphia and Cleveland. He
thought of all the streets and all the houses, the public
buildings and the crisscross of iron rails, aqueducts, docks

and bridges, of the arsenal, of schools and colleges and the penitentiary. Here were people, people, people, thousands of people doing thousands of jobs.

Among all those people, who could be expected to provide bread for the Meyer table and shoes for the Meyer feet? Not one.

"Mama's right," Otto told Katherine. "I'll have to quit school and find a job."

"Not now," Katherine begged. "In three weeks school will be out. You have good marks. You will be promoted. Oh, Otto!" She stopped in the middle of the sidewalk and threw her arms around his waist. "You *must* finish school. Papa worked so hard to learn to read and speak English. You can't quit now. We'll be all right. It must take more than three weeks to starve!"

"You aren't going to starve," Otto said gruffly, but he heaved a great sigh of relief. "All right, Trinka. I won't quit."

Suddenly Otto became aware of the dozens of children hurrying toward school. Three girls walked the curbing to go around Otto and Katherine. They giggled. The boys who followed hooted. Otto stepped out of the circle of his sister's comforting arms. Blackly he scowled at both Katherine and the boys who booed. He ordered curtly, "Cut it out, Trinka!"

Tears spilled down Katherine's round cheeks, but she made no sound. Her chin raised, her shoulders squared, she marched across the gravelled schoolyard with the same fierce courage she had shown in the churchyard. Otto wanted to run after her, but he let her go on alone.

On The Stranger's Mountain

In his classroom Otto found that review for final examinations had begun. Otto was a good student. He took pride in his work. From the day he entered first grade, Papa had built dreams for him. "Someday, Otto," Papa would say, "you will have a fine education. You will go to the high school, then to Mr. Carnegie's Institute. I will work very hard. I will give you this chance I did not have."

One day Papa scrubbed the coal dust from his hands and fingernails and took Otto and Katherine to see the Carnegie Institute. Papa said an iron-and-steel master had given the library, museum, art gallery, music hall and school to the people. Aglow with the wonder of all the books and all the paintings, Papa cried, "This man! This man sees more than dust and smoke in Pittsburgh. He sees the *people* who make his steel. It is important to see the people."

That day Papa bought popcorn and ice-cream cones, rare treats for the Meyer children. They tramped the gullies and ridges, and even rode to the end of the streetcar line. They looked at houses and offices and mills, at schools and hospitals and fire stations. They looked at the city. But most of all, they looked at the people.

Papa tapped his skull and said, "It is up here that a man is free. I want that for my children. Freedom! Not everybody knows how to be free. I think you will learn something about it in books, but you will learn more by living."

At last they returned to the house they rented from Big Mike. Papa shouted in German when Mama opened the door, "On this day I have opened a door for my children! I have shown them how to be American!" He kissed Mama's

34

forehead and the soft spot under her chin, and Mama said, "Yes, Johann, that is good." Mama did not understand what Papa was talking about. She did not understand about Papa's dream for his children.

Now the door had closed. If Mama opened it, a stranger would stand on the steps, a stranger named Bela Karl Czek, who shook hands when he made promises.

4

Pickles for Mr. Heinz

The days that followed were not easy. Otto found odd jobs in the neighborhood. Often he worked until midnight, only to tramp up the steep street and up the many steps, to sleep a few hours, to go to school, then to work again.

"You will make yourself sick," Mama scolded, but her voice was gentle. Sometimes Otto wished she would order him to quit school, but she did not. For the first time in her life Mama walked over the ridge to the post office every day. Each day she came home with little to say.

When Otto came home from sweeping out a tavern, or scrubbing Big Mike's meat-cutting slab, or uncrating canned goods for Vito's hole-in-the-wall grocery store, he would find Mama counting Papa's money. Pastor Schmidt sat with her almost every day. He brought offerings of food from the congregation. These Mama took with a childlike murmur of gratitude and downcast eyes. Otto knew she was not thinking about the food. She was thinking about the letter and the money.

No coins remained when the rent was paid to Big Mike.

Pickles for Mr. Heinz

On that day Mama's eyes were red when she came home from the post office.

The next day when Otto came home from school, he found the door locked. He rattled the knob. He heard a scraping sound. Hans pulled a chair to the window and climbed up to peep out through the curtains. "Unlock the door, Hansel," Otto coaxed.

Hans put his mouth close to the glass as if to push his words through the pane to Otto. He said, "Mama said don't let anybody in."

Patiently Otto explained, "I'm not anybody. I belong here."

Hans sucked his thumb while he considered. Katherine, Martin and Gussie joined Otto on the porch. They, too, coaxed and smiled. At last Hans climbed from his chair and unlatched the door.

The minute the door opened Katherine demanded, "Where's Mama?"

"She . . . she . . ." Hans gave up and dropped hands to his sides. His round eyes flooded, his mouth puckered.

"Ssh, ssh," Katherine comforted. "It's all right, Hansel. You were a good boy to keep the door locked."

"Weren't you scared?" Gussie asked solemnly. At that, Hans broke into a loud bellow.

Katherine flew to put her arms around the small boy. Reproachfully she told Gussie, "Augustus Meyer! You shouldn't have reminded him."

"I'd have been scared," Gussie insisted.

After the three rooms had been minutely inspected, then once again, Martin whimpered, "I want Mama. I feel sick."

"You're just hungry," Katherine told him.

"If I build the fire, can you make potato soup?" Otto asked Katherine. "I have to work in a print shop down on the riverfront."

Katherine lifted her chin. She said, "I'll manage."

Tom-the-printer kept a dark, cluttered shop near the end of a bridge. After Otto left the hillside community where he lived and found most of his work, he hurried through a tunnel. He tried not to foresee the blackness that would fill this space before he finished counting and bundling handbills.

While he worked, Otto tried to guess what Mama was doing. Once he thought of Martin's pale face. He could almost hear Papa say, "If there's one thing we can do without, it's sickness."

Then Tom set Otto to nailing etched zinc plates on inch-thick blocks. The task was so painstaking, Otto forgot to worry. The evening seemed unbearably long. He was hungry. Usually Mama gave him boiled beans and rye bread before he went to work. Tonight, since she was out, he had eaten nothing.

"Time to sweep up," said Tom-the-printer. Otto attacked the print shop clutter.

Suddenly Otto was struck by a chilling thought. Maybe that *man*, that Mr. Check, had come from Denver!

"No," he told himself. "No, I didn't mention marriage in the letter. He wouldn't come. No." The more he argued with himself, the harder Otto swept.

Pickles for Mr. Heinz

Tom-the-printer yelled, "Watch it, Ott! You just missed my type case. If you pi my type, I'll kick your hip pockets through your backbone!"

"Yes, sir," Otto mumbled nervously.

Otto was glad when Tom-the-printer flipped a quarter into the air, caught it and tossed it on the counter. "Night, Ott. I'll get in touch when I need you." Tom pulled his green eyeshade over bulging, pale eyes and bent over his type case. He did not look up when Otto let himself into the street.

Fog horns mooed on the river. Searchlights pushed anxious fingers this way and that way, revealing night-crawling barges. The tunnel was longer and blacker than Otto had imagined. He heard his own footsteps, the echo, then the echo of the echo. His teeth chattered by the time he came out of the tunnel and heard the haunting chant of voices at a Negro church on the waterfront.

Hungry and tired though he was, Otto ran all the steep way home. With a mounting sense of panic he climbed the long stairs to the front porch.

Was a man in the house? Had Mr. Check come from Denver?

Then he heard Mama's voice. Though he could not understand each separate word, he was reassured by the familiar cadence of spoken German. Mama was brushing Katherine's hair.

Otto leaned his head on the unpainted porch post until he felt calm. Then he opened the door and went in.

With a puzzled frown Mama asked, "Is something wrong, Otto?"

39

Wrong or right, Otto did not know. He knew only that Papa's friend, Mr. Check, was not in the house. He had not come in person to answer that letter. Otto said, "No, Mama."

Katherine went to bed and Mama dished up Otto's potato soup. She added a thick slab of rye bread and a slice of cheese. Then she sat at the table with her arms folded on the oilcloth. Otto gave Mama his quarter. Hungrily, he ate.

Severely Mama said, "You cannot keep this up. You are losing flesh from your bones, and you have none to spare."

"School will soon be out. Then I can work all day," Otto said. "I'll have to. Papa's money is gone."

"I know," Mama agreed, "so I got a job. I will not wait for Mr. Czek."

Otto clattered his spoon in amazement. "A job, Mama? Where?" This was unbelievable. Mama knew nothing of jobs. When she crossed the river, someone had to go with her to interpret. Mama spoke no English. How could she find and hold a job?

"In the cannery," Mama explained. "I will make pickles for Mr. Heinz." Pride, fear, and a hint of self-confidence colored Mama's cheeks and brightened her blue eyes, but Otto noticed that she twisted the heavy gold wedding band. She spoke too breathlessly and rapidly.

Otto had been born in this neighborhood. Still, he feared. He did not want Mama to run through the dark, as he had run tonight. "I will take your place. I will make the pickles," he offered earnestly.

"No," Mama said.

40

Before Otto could argue his point with Mama, Martin cried.

Mama jumped up from the table. With Otto at her heels, she ran to the crowded bedroom. In the dim light, she pushed through the narrow space between Hans' crib and the foot of the double bed she now shared with Katherine.

Papa had built shelves on a wall. These served as bunks for Martin and Gussie. Martin slept nearest the ceiling. Mama gathered him into her arms and carried him to the kitchen. "Tell me," she crooned, "what is wrong?"

Martin squirmed with pain. He tried to fight his way out of her arms.

Otto cleared the kitchen table. Mama laid Martin on the flat surface. Martin rocked and twisted. "I hurt, Mama," he cried. "I hurt!"

Mama's fingers probed the area around Martin's ears, his throat, his chest, and his stomach. When she touched his right side, perspiration burst through his pores. His eyes glazed with pain.

"Fix a hot water bottle, please, Otto," Mama ordered.

With trembling fingers, Otto filled the red rubber bottle and screwed in the black cork. Wrapped in a towel, the bottle was placed on Martin's abdomen.

"Heat blankets," Mama said.

Otto stripped the blankets from his own cot and draped them on the chairs before the open oven door. He opened dampers and set fire to the coals in the range.

Mama stayed beside Martin, urging him to sip water, to lie quietly, to "sleep, little one, sleep."

Martin could not sleep. The blankets were only temporary

41

relief. Katherine awoke and joined Mama in the kitchen. Even Gussie, the six-year-old, climbed from his shelf bed to see what was going on in the kitchen.

"Go back to bed, Gussie. I must have room to move quickly when Martin needs me," Mama told the sleepy boy.

Gussie obeyed, but unwillingly.

"We need a doctor," Katherine declared.

"You know we have no money!" Mama cried out. She worked twice as hard to soothe Martin's pain.

At the end of an hour Otto whispered to Katherine, "Keep the fire going. I'll go for help."

Otto stumbled down the many steps and through the steep, twisting streets and alleys till he came to Big Mike's house. He knocked long and loudly. He roused nobody.

He had better luck at the Rubino house. "Whatsa wrong? Is a fire?" Vito shouted into the dark. Instantly a light showed around the edges of a green cloth window shade. The kitchen light came through a window and onto the porch. Otto stood in the middle of the square of light.

When Vito opened the door he said, "Oh, itsa Otto. What can I do?" In long-legged underwear, the short Italian leaned against a doorpost. He scrubbed thick black hair to shake sleep from his eyes, then scratched his ribs.

Otto explained about Martin and the pain that would not go away.

"Maria!" Vito shouted, not caring that his shout brought the small Rubinos from their beds. They huddled around Vito in the open doorway.

Plump Maria padded into the kitchen. Barefoot, she clutched the neck of a long flannel nightgown.

In rapid, musical words Otto did not understand, Vito explained the situation to Maria. Both waved arms and flicked fingers. Then Vito told Otto, "Maria, she come. I go for police." He shushed all the young Rubinos and said, "Bambinos, stay."

With a cotton dress pulled over her flannel nightgown and braids flapping her shoulders, Mrs. Rubino hurried back up the hill with Otto. They found Mama in the rocking chair with Martin in her arms.

Mrs. Rubino spoke no German; Mama spoke no Italian. Voices rose as each tried to make herself understood. Martin stirred and cried out. Mama patted his cheek while she shouted.

"Did she give him castor oil?" Maria asked Otto. "Itsa bad, oil. A neighbor I had once. He tooka the oil. He died."

"No," Otto choked. "No oil, unless . . ." Fearfully he turned to Katherine.

She said, "No, no oil."

"The heat she is bad, too, I think. We needa doctor," Maria shouted. She tried to remove the hot water bottle. Mama clutched Martin. Martin cried.

In the middle of the hubbub Vito pushed open the kitchen door. He was followed by one of the policemen who had attended Papa's funeral. "I broughta police," Vito declared.

"Police?" Mama cried in German. Frightened eyes demanded an explanation from Otto.

The uniformed man tried to examine the small boy on Mama's lap. She held Martin close and demanded fiercely, "Is it a crime to be sick?"

44

"What did she say?" the Irish policeman asked. When Otto told him, he said, "Tell your mother I'll take the boy to the hospital. I'm sure he has appendicitis. Probably he needs an operation."

Otto tried to make Mama understand. She moaned. She held Martin so closely the policeman unlocked her fingers by force. The man said gently, "I'm sorry. I know this is hard on your mother, but this boy needs help."

5

He Drank Tea!

The Irish policeman and Vito Rubino locked hands to make a stretcher. They carried Martin out of the house and down the long stairs. When they reached the steep street, Otto ran alongside. He made sure Martin's blanket stayed in place. Katherine remained with Gussie and Hans. Mama fought off Maria Rubino's hands. She stumbled and shouted at the end of the little procession.

At Vito's grocery store, the policeman called for an ambulance. When he heard the siren, Otto stiffened with fright. He asked, "What shall I do?"

The policeman advised, "Better stay with your mother, son. She needs you. Martin will be in good hands. Dr. Wong will patch him up, good as new."

Everybody in the riverfront slums knew Dr. Wong's name. "Dr. Wong," "Charity," and "Hospital" were three words as inseparable as the Three Wise Men.

"No!" Mama protested. "I will take Martin home. I will take care of him. Don't send him away to the hospital to die!" Mama clung to the policeman's arm while she pleaded.

The policeman turned to Otto to ask what Mama was saying. Almost crossly he told Otto, "Tell her nobody is going to harm Martin. We'll take good care of him. Dr. Wong will make him well."

Two men with white uniforms put Martin in the ambulance and drove away. Mama refused to speak to the policeman.

"If only I could make you people understand that you don't have to suffer alone." The policeman wiped his forehead with his handkerchief. "We have a program of public assistance, visiting nurses, a clinic, a ward at the hospital. If you will report your need, we will see that you don't suffer."

Mama spoke no English. She did not understand a word the policeman said. Otto was hungry, tired, sleepy, and confused by the suddenness of Martin's illness. Otto nodded solemnly while the policeman talked, but the words did not go inside his ears. He knew only that other people had left the hillside to go to Dr. Wong's hospital. Sometimes they lived, sometimes they died.

After the ambulance carried Martin beyond sight and touch, Otto walked up the hill with Mama. For half a block Maria Rubino trotted beside Mama. Maria crooned and comforted. Mama neither understood nor listened. Maria went home.

When Otto and Mama entered the kitchen, they found Katherine in a wooden chair with her arithmetic book in her lap. Soberly she told Otto, "I'm studying my multiplication tables. The sevens and nines are hard. I can't think of anything else when I say them."

"To bed," Mama said.

The next morning Mama did not go to the cannery to

make pickles. Otto, Katherine and Gussie did not go to school. They sat. Silently, soberly, they sat around the oilcloth-covered table, hands folded, waiting.

Quite early in the morning a policeman brought a woman who asked questions and wrote answers on a paper. She said brightly, "I'll keep in touch. Martin had an emergency appendectomy. He is a husky little boy. He will make a quick recovery."

Otto and Katherine tried to tell Mama what the woman had said, but they did not know the German words. Mama could not grasp the English words. They sat helplessly. After a while the policeman took Mama to sit with Martin. He explained, "So he won't be afraid."

"I'd better go with Mama so *she* won't be afraid," Katherine said wisely.

Otto stayed home with Gussie and Hans. A man came to the door. He told Otto, "Your name has been turned in at my office. There's been a death in your family?"

Otto said, "Yes, sir," and explained that Mama was not at home.

The man walked through the house. He looked at the beds and the coal bin. He opened the cupboard doors. He wrote on a paper and went away.

Otto's cheeks burned with embarrassment when the opened doors revealed so little food. It upset him that strangers paraded through the house. Neighbors brought food——a pot of soup, a loaf of hot bread. Big Mike sent a whole salami, but not even Gussie felt like eating.

At noon Mrs. Rubino brought a big copper pot filled with hot, fragrant food. She lifted the lid to let steam rise in

Otto's face. She said briskly, "Pasto. Food. Eat." She lifted three plates from a shelf and dished up great mounds of spaghetti, juicy with sauce. With both hands on her wide hips, Maria stood at the table to see that Otto, Gussie and Hans ate.

Otto was washing the plates and forks when he heard a knock. Having eaten Maria's hot "pasto," Otto felt braver. He determined not to allow another person to open Mama's cupboard doors. When he opened the front door, he stood squarely in the middle of the threshold, barring passageway.

A very tall man in a blue serge suit asked, "Is this the home of Mrs. Johann Meyer?"

"Yes, sir," Otto answered. He waited for the questions that would follow.

The man held a hat in his hands. The hat was larger than Otto had seen on the heads of men on the streets of Pittsburgh. Otto kept his eyes on the hat, aware that the man looked over his head into the room beyond the open door.

"Is Mrs. Meyer at home?" the man asked, after a silence.

"No, sir," Otto admitted.

"When may I see her?" the tall man asked.

"Are you from the hospital?" Otto asked uneasily. "How . . . how is Martin?"

Otto sensed that he had startled the man, but all the stranger said was, "Have you trouble?"

Trouble! Otto had carried his full load of trouble since the night Papa did not come home. "Y-yes, sir," he said.

The man moved away from the door. With loose-jointed ease he leaned against a porch post. He fished a cloth tobacco sack and a package of brown papers from his pocket. Carefully he took out one paper, dumped in a tiny pile of ground tobacco, rolled and twisted the cigarette. With a quick flick of his tongue he sealed the cigarette, then lighted a wooden match with one thumbnail. With much concentration he puffed and inhaled. When a smoke ring hit the air, he said, "Tell me about it."

Without invitation he sat on the edge of the porch.

Something about the man encouraged confidence. Otto sat. For a while he said nothing. He stared out over twisting streets, flights of wooden stairs, rock-piled walls, and soot-grimed buildings that hunched one behind the other above the steel mills on the only flat land. Smokestacks filled the sky above the valley. Each puffed white-hot smoke. As the smoke cooled, it darkened.

The man pointed his cigarette at the mills. He asked, "Did your father work down there?"

"No, sir," Otto said. "He dug coal." He could almost hear Papa say proudly, "For this I dig the coal — to make the steel!"

"And there was an accident?" the man prompted.

"Yes, sir."

"You don't talk much, do you, son?" the man asked. When Otto looked into the tall man's face, he saw smile lines settle around gray eyes and wide mouth. A scar in his hairline was surrounded by a patch of white. The rest of the hair was brown, thick and slightly curly. Otto noticed with approval that the man's neck was clean.

"It's Martin," Otto said. With a rush he told about the night and day of confusion. Once in a while the man asked a question or repeated a word. Otto found himself telling about Papa and Katherine's wreath and Mama's strange letter, about his after-school jobs and the pickles Mama planned to make for Mr. Heinz.

"Shouldn't you be in school?" the man asked.

Otto's mouth dropped open. Still another fright leaped into his mind. This man must be the dreaded truant officer! Mama was at the hospital. If Otto was taken away by the truant officer, who would stay with Gussie and Hans?

With desperate earnestness Otto promised, "I'll go to-morrow."

"See that you do," the man advised. He stood up and settled the big felt hat on his brown hair. "I'll be back tomorrow."

Otto watched the tall man go down the long flight of stairs. He did not go toward the huddle of stores, but turned toward the river. Otto thought the man must be checking up on boys who fished, when they should be in school.

Soon Mama and Katherine appeared at the foot of the steep street. Otto shut the door to keep Hans and Gussie from following. He hurried down the hillside stairs to meet Mama. He called anxiously, "Martin?"

"He smiled at us!" Katherine called back. "He drank tea!"

"Tea!" Otto repeated, overcome with happiness that Martin could open his lips to drink tea.

Together Mama, Katherine, and Otto returned to the crowded little house. Katherine had much to say about the rows of clean white beds, the nurses and Dr. Wong, and the ride in the police car. Otto forgot to tell about

the man who opened the cupboard doors. Not even the truant officer seemed important at the moment.

Otto kept his promise to the stranger. He went back to school the next day. Katherine felt she must go to the hospital with Mama. Gussie had missed Martin, especially at night, since the shelf bed above his own was empty. Mama allowed Gussie to visit Martin, too, but both Katherine and Gussie returned to school in the afternoon. In the early evening Otto saw the stranger climb the stairs. He shouted, "You don't need to come up. We went to school!"

Still climbing, the man answered, "I'll just visit with your mother for a spell."

"She isn't home," Otto called back. "She's making pickles for Mr. Heinz. She's on the night shift."

"That right?" The man sounded puzzled. He took off his big hat and rubbed the white hair around his scar. Then he said, "I thought she didn't speak English."

"She doesn't," Otto explained, "but the shift boss is Mr. Bauer. He can tell Mama what to do."

"Oh, that's good," the visitor said. A little awkwardly he added, "I think."

Martin spent ten days in the hospital, ten of the busiest days of Otto's life. At school Otto struggled with final examinations. After three-thirty he dusted books for the whisper-voiced librarian, picked up pins and swept the floor for Israel Fishbein, the tailor, or washed butcher shop windows. Since Mama worked at night, Otto and Katherine divided the work at home.

Mama was cheerful most of the time now, but very quiet. One day she arrived home from work an hour late. Though she seemed to have been crying, her eyes shone. When Katherine asked Mama what troubled her, Mama said, "I spoke with a friend, an old friend. I was surprised to see . . ."

Otto thought Mama said "him." Mama slurred the word. Otto was not thinking in German and might have missed her meaning. He shrugged to dismiss the fleeting impression he had received that Mama might have seen Bela Czek.

For a few days Otto listened more closely when Mama spoke, and he checked the clock to see what time she came home from work. She was never late. There was no mention of old friends.

There was less worry now. A supply of food and coal had been delivered like gifts from heaven. More was promised, though Otto failed to understand how this could be.

Each day at dusk the stranger with the pleasant voice and the big hat came to the door. Each time he started back down the long stairs he asked, "Sure you're not afraid to stay alone?"

"We're fine," Katherine or Otto or Gussie would say. Even Hans stood in a chair to wave at the tall man, and looked wistful when he disappeared at the foot of the steep street.

"He's the oddest truant officer I ever heard of," Otto mused.

"He's nice," Katherine declared. "I like him."

6

About That River

The day Otto, Katherine, and Gussie received their report cards and carried home their school supplies, Martin came home from the hospital. White, thin, and very, very clean, he sat in Papa's wooden rocking chair in the living room.

Katherine demanded of the whole family, "Isn't Martin pretty?" She stood in front of Martin and beamed.

"Don't call me pretty," Martin objected. "Boys aren't pretty."

"What are they?" Hans wanted to know.

Katherine declared positively, "When they look like Martin, boys are pretty!" With a flourish she opened her arithmetic book and brought out a brown envelope. "Here's your report card," she told Martin. "You passed! You're in fourth grade now."

"We all passed," Otto said gladly.

"Oh."

All eyes turned to Gussie, who had made the dismal exclamation.

"Gussie, what do you mean, 'oh?'" Otto asked.

Gussie's lips drooped at the corners. He scrubbed one

foot across the bare floor. "I mean that nice truant man won't come to see us anymore, 'cause school's out."

"That's right," Katherine said, turning sober.

This was Otto's evening to deliver handbills for Tom-the-printer. As he went up, down and around through the crooked streets, he thought about the man whose gray eyes were framed by smile lines; thought about him so hard he was not surprised to find the man sitting on a stone wall.

"What are you doing?" Otto asked.

"Looking," the man said, "and thinking."

Otto stopped beside the man. He laid his bundle of handbills on the stone wall. To his surprise Otto looked down on the backyard and roof of his own home. "Do you come up here often?" he asked uneasily. Otto had come to like the man, in spite of his fear of truant officers. He added, "I suppose this is a good place to see who's playing hookey."

Smile crinkles deepened. The man repeated solemnly, "Oh, yes. Hookey. From school."

"What do you do when school's out?" Otto asked.

The man waited so long to answer, Otto thought he might have asked a question that was none of his business. His thin cheeks flushed with embarrassment.

"I wasn't thinking about school," the man said. "I was thinking about some mountains out west, and a river." He jerked a thumb at the Monongahela where barges crawled and bawled. "My river runs clean. There's no smoke in the air. There is grass to walk on, enough to feed a flock of sheep and a herd of cattle, with enough left over for the mule deer. The houses are ten, twenty, fifty miles apart. You want to go some place, you ride a horse and take along your grubstake. You take your time, out there on my mountain. There's no one around to raise a ruckus."

"Oh—h."

"You like the sound of it, Otto?"

"Oh, yes, sir," Otto breathed.

"If I had a bunch of kids, that's where I'd take them," the man said. Without another word he put his feet on the ground and walked away.

Otto felt lonely, watching him disappear in a gully. For a moment, while the man talked, Otto had left the slums. He had sat astride a tall horse on the stranger's mountain.

As the hard weeks passed, the stranger's mountain and Papa's plan of progress blended. In Otto's mind they mixed like the Monongahela and the Allegheny, joining to form the Ohio River.

Otto needed his private dream. The summer was unusually hot. Mama worked on the night shift at the cannery. The children learned to tiptoe and whisper till noon to allow Mama to sleep. During the midday they helped her to wash, iron, bake bread, boil beans and stews and heat bath water.

Mama was strangely restless and no longer asked if a letter had come from Bela Czek, Papa's friend who shook hands when he made promises.

Each night when Mama went to work she cautioned, "Don't build a fire. This house is an oven, with the sun and the coal range both going all day!" It became a ritual for Mama to call from the bottom of the hillside stairs, "Remember, Otto, you're the man of the house."

Undersized and thin though he was, Otto accepted that responsibility like a pack on his back. He found daytime work in order to spend the evening hours with the younger children. Mama left the house before black dark. When she came home in the early morning, the streets were deserted. Otto hoped she was not afraid. As for himself, he was glad he did not have to pass through the tunnel at midnight. In daytime that tunnel was only a concrete tube.

Otto had very little trouble with the younger children. While Papa lived they had looked up to "Big Brother." They respected his position as "man of the house." They worked, too, and helped Mama in every possible way.

Evening hours were the hardest. Loneliness crept in with the shadows. After their cold supper Otto, Katherine, Martin, Gussie and Hans lined up on the narrow front porch or sat on the steps on the wooden hillside stairs. Patiently they waited for the stir of the first evening breeze down the old "Mon."

They played simple sit-down games, sang every song they knew, told and retold their fund of stories. Katherine was best at storytelling, but one hot night even she ran out of ideas.

"It's your turn to tell a story, Otto," Katherine said.

Otto gulped. He looked at the boys' waiting faces. He looked down on other houses, other stairs, all lined with people waiting for the coolness. Suddenly he thought with longing of the stranger's mountain.

"Remember the man who used to knock on the door after Mama went to work?" Otto asked.

"The truant officer," Gussie said promptly.

59

"He told me about a mountain and a river," Otto began. As he repeated the man's words, the story tangled with one of his own imagining. With clenched fists Otto dreamed aloud of that life beside a clean river. With every nerve in his thin body, Otto wanted to climb Papa's ladder, and it seemed possible when he talked about the river. To give his family a future and a chance, Otto must give up his own boyhood. He must sacrifice his own playtime and training years. He was doomed to nothingness and knew it. It hurt his heart, but he did not complain. He was grateful for the stranger's dream. It gave him something to think about.

"Can't you tell us more?" Martin asked. "I like those mountains."

"And the sheep and cows," Gussie said.

"An' the mule deer," Hans piped. Then he asked, "Whatsa mule deer?"

"Some kind of animal," Otto said.

"Katrinka could go to the library and find out," Martin suggested. "She could bring home a book about that river. I'd take care of Gussie and Hans."

Spiritedly Gussie retorted, "You mean we'd take care of you." Martin had not completely regained his strength. He was "taken care of" by the whole family.

As the summer passed, the stranger's dream became their own. Katherine carried home books from the library. She read aloud about the land that lay west of the Mississippi. The five looked at maps and pictures. They tried to guess which big river the stranger had meant.

About That River

The Columbia? Colorado? Platte, Missouri, Yellowstone? Gila? Musselshell?

Katherine thought it must be the Columbia; Martin, the Colorado. Even Hans chose a river to claim as his own. Pursing his lips and nodding wisely, he would say, "It's the Green river." Hans knew his colors. He could understand a river named Green.

Otto reminded, "Remember, there are mountains and grass. Some of those rivers run through flat prairies."

"I don't know about prairies," Hans declared. "I know green."

Otto did not know about prairies, either, but he read the books handed out by the whisper-voiced librarian. He flushed with pleasure when she said, "Your papa would be so happy about your choice of reading material. He was an unusual man, your papa. Not every immigrant has the courage to educate himself."

"He had a dream," Otto confided, in the low voice that fitted the atmosphere of the library.

"I know," the librarian whispered. "He used to tell me about it. He said his children have a ladder to climb to get from the place where they are to the place where he wanted them to be. He had to provide that ladder. He wanted a good, strong ladder on a firm foundation, so he studied, all by himself, in a language foreign to him. He wanted to know how to choose the ladder."

The librarian wiped her eyes. "We need more men like your papa, Otto," she said.

Otto tiptoed from the library, carrying his books. At the

double glass door he looked back. He saw the librarian stoop to whisper to another child checking out a book. Plain, middle-aged, almost voiceless, she was not a person to be noticed in a group, but Otto was aware of a debt he owed her; first, for the help she had given Papa, and second, for the gift she had just bestowed. This gift was an unexpected picture of Papa as he had looked to other people.

As Otto walked home he opened a book about the wild animals of the great Northwest. He must tell Hans about the mule deer. Watching traffic and leafing through the book, Otto wondered if Papa had sometimes dreamed of a mountain beside a clean river.

In the year that followed the young Meyers had much need for both Papa's dream and the stranger's mountain. Mama continued to work at the cannery where her "boss" and "crew" spoke German. She absolutely refused to permit the children to speak one word of English in her presence. She had no natural gift for languages, so made no effort to fit into the neighborhood.

Mama did not learn about money. Papa had handled the money while he lived. Now she left the responsibility to Otto.

"These bills, these checks," she said, fluttering her hands. "I do not understand."

Otto changed her small wages into coins Mama could count. He kept an anxious eye on the old teapot she used for a bank.

More than once Katherine said impatiently, "I wish Mama would grow up!"

Otto agreed, but as "man of the house" he could allow no criticism of Mama, even when she stumbled through life more dependent than Hans.

There were bright spots in the dreary days. From some source Otto could not discover, money came to pay for fuel and for shoes. A grocery wagon brought a huge turkey for Thanksgiving. They enjoyed it as long as a bone was left for soup.

A box of books, clothing and toys arrived during the Christmas holidays. On the flyleaf of Otto's book was written, "Knowledge will help you climb that ladder."

Mama did not seem surprised to receive the Christmas box, but Otto was puzzled. He carried his book to the whisper-voiced librarian.

She knew nothing about the gift. Shifting his feet with embarrassment, Otto said, "I thought you might have told the Welfare people about Papa's dream."

"Oh, no!" The librarian forgot to whisper. "Charity is not a part of that dream!"

Otto raised his chin and smiled. He said, "Thank you." Her words helped him to make the decision he had put off too long. He went to the Welfare office and announced, "You will please send no more money to the Johann Meyer family. I will quit school. I will get a job. I will pay for my family's coal and shoes."

The gray-haired woman behind the desk looked through

files. Then she told Otto, "The Johann Meyer family is not listed with us. Might some other name have been used?"

"Mrs. Anna Meyer?" Otto suggested.

Again she fingered the cards. She said, "No, not Mrs. Anna Meyer."

"Maybe the welfare comes to me. I am the man of the family," Otto said.

"No," the woman told Otto. "I am sure your family is not listed."

"But, where . . ." Otto began.

"I am sure I do not know what makes you think you are receiving our aid," the woman said. "If you are managing to get along, by whatever means, please, don't quit school."

"I won't," Otto said breathlessly. He walked home with his thoughts all a-whirl. Since his family was not on a charity list, who could be helping Mama? Pastor Schmidt, maybe?

Otto talked to the Pastor, but that good man said, "No, the church has sent nothing since last summer. A man came to my office and said he would be responsible for the needs of the Johann Meyer family."

In amazement Otto asked, "A man? Who is he?"

"I am not free to tell you," Pastor said. He put one hand on Otto's thin shoulder as he said, "He is an honorable man with a generous heart. This I can tell you, my son. No more."

Otto even ventured to ask Mama if she had any idea of the man's identity.

"Man?" Mama repeated, wide-eyed as Hans. "Paying for our coal? How can this be? I work! I make pickles for Mr. Heinz. I pay!"

"Yes, Mama," Otto said gently, then said nothing more. But each time the coal bin was refilled or a case of canned food or a sack of flour was delivered for Mama's loaves, he wondered. Who had paid?

Even with the help from the "honorable man" there were no luxuries in the Meyer house. The milk they drank came from a can. Their clothing was mended and passed from boy to boy. Darning the stockings was Katherine's chore. She sewed on buttons and mended the knees and elbows of knickers and jackets.

One dresser with three drawers held the whole family's clothing. One small cupboard and a tiny dugout cellar held their food. The coal bin was a wooden box on the narrow back porch. Each day Otto looked at the dresser, the cupboard and the bin before he went to school. If something was needed, he stayed out for the day and found an odd job. Though his attendance record was spotted with A's for "absent," the rest of the A's on his report card were marks of excellence. Otto was a good student. He liked school, and treasured each day, knowing it could be his last.

Somehow, they got through that long, hard year and summer came again.

On the hottest day of August, Mama sent Katherine to the branch post office. She said, "There might be a letter from Uncle Ernst or Aunt Berta. Gussie, you're to sweep the porches. Martin, see that Hans doesn't fall on the hill-stairs.

65

And, Otto . . ." Mama stared at Otto. She asked with disapproval, "Why are you not working?"

"No one needed me today," Otto explained. Hastily he added when Mama frowned, "But I have two jobs for tomorrow!"

"The windows need washing," Mama said. She went back to the ironing board in the hot kitchen. Otto filled a pail with hot, soapy water and set to work.

At the end of an hour Mama sat on the front porch to cool off. She fanned herself with her starched apron while Otto washed the cracked panes of the "front room" windows. They saw Katherine appear at the foot of the steep street. She was running.

Katherine climbed the hill-stairs so fast Mama shouted, "Katrinka, sit! You will have heat stroke, running in this sun."

"A letter, a letter!" Katherine shrieked. "And it isn't from Germany."

Mama stopped fanning while she stared downhill at Katherine. "It's not from—from Mr. . . . ."

"Yes, it is," Katherine panted. "It's from Mr. Check."

Hearing the man's name, Otto spilled soapy water. He stood in the middle of the puddle, helplessly wiggling his toes. Fifteen months ago he had written the letter for Mama. After all this time, why had Mr. Check written?

Feeling sick, Otto stared from Mama to the letter Katherine held.

7

'Board!

Mama's cheeks, ears, and even the back of her neck burned red as she sat with Mr. Check's letter in her hands. Tears spilled from her blue eyes. She did not try to wipe them. She suffered in some adult way beyond Otto's experience.

That suffering pushed aside Otto's own feeling of angry helplessness. Gently he said, "Shall I read your letter to you, Mama?"

She nodded her blond, braid-wrapped head. Silently she handed the letter to Otto. The tears continued to spill over her cheeks while his fingers fumbled to tear open the envelope.

Making stiff conversation, Katherine said, "He writes very neatly."

"Yes," Otto agreed, as politely as one answers a stranger.

When he opened the single sheet, Otto saw that the letter was written in German and dated August 13, 1922. In a tight, squeaky voice, unsuited to the phrasing of the letter, Otto read:

To Mrs. Johann Meyer, Anna, my friend: It grieved me to hear of the death of Johann, your husband and my friend. I remember him with warmth.

Since I have never married, I am free to honor the contract we made in 1909. I propose marriage and promise to raise Johann's children as my own.

At the time I received your letter, I was unable to fit a family into my small house. I have provided space.

I enclose a money order to cover the expenses of your trip. If my offer meets with your approval, I will await you in Grangeville, Idaho, on September 4.

I remain your obedient servant, Bela Karl Czek.

While Otto read, the three younger boys crowded against Mama to listen, wide-eyed and grave. Katherine stared down on the smokestacks of the steel mills. Mama pleated her starched apron with work-reddened hands.

When Otto pronounced the last word, a silence grew. After a while each Meyer stirred nervously, reluctant to speak first.

It was Mama who said, "This Idaho, where is it?"

"It's . . ." Otto began. Puzzled, he looked at Mama, unable to explain the geography of the United States of America to Mama. Her world extended from a three-room shack to the pickle factory. A few houses in Germany lay in some dim place on the fringe of that world. Mama shut her eyes to life beyond her own four walls.

"It's one of the Northwestern states," Katherine said.

"Is there a river?" Gussie asked. He had fastened his attention on the familiar word "western."

"I'll bring the book," Hans offered. He trotted into the house and brought back the book that contained the most maps. He spread Katherine's geography book on the porch floor. Martin, Gussie and Hans dropped to knees to hunch over the bright maps.

"There's green." Hans pointed at a map.

Martin, who had been promoted to the fifth grade, frowned at the patch of green. He said, "But it isn't a river."

"Oh," Hans said. Green paper, green river, it was green. Hans understood green.

Abruptly Mama stood up. She said, "We must pack. Soon comes September 4."

Feeling hot, cold, hot, cold, Otto clenched his fists. He begged, "Don't do this thing, Mama. We are getting along all right. We have food. There's coal in the bin and . . ."

"We go," Mama said.

"You have the job at the cannery," Otto pleaded. "And I'll work! I'll quit school. I'll . . ." To Otto's dismay he burst into tears, sobbing aloud as he talked.

In promising to leave school, he had offered his biggest sacrifice. It was not accepted. He could do no more.

When he could not stop crying, Otto ran into the house and slammed the door. In the little shoebox living room, Otto threw himself on his cot and gave way to hysteria. He felt Mama's hand on his shoulders, patting, patting. He rolled free of her hands. He cried out, "Go away! You've forgotten Papa!"

"No, Otto," Mama said. "I am remembering Papa. I am keeping a promise I made."

"I don't understand!" Otto sobbed wildly. Mama's hands stopped patting. He heard her go into the bedroom and shut the door. Smaller hands touched his back. Katherine said softly, "It will work out all right, Otto. You and I will manage."

"We can't," Otto cried. "Mr. Check won't let us."

"Maybe he will be a *little* bit like Papa," Katherine said, hesitantly.

"How can you say that?" Otto demanded fiercely. "He wrote in German, didn't he?"

Not even to Katherine could Otto explain his pride in Papa's effort to become American, or his feeling that Papa was not dead but just "away." Otto knew Papa would never come back, but Papa's warm presence in Otto's memory gave the boy the courage to be the "man of the family."

With the coming of another man, Papa would disappear. Then, how could Otto place Papa's ladder for the Meyer feet to climb? Mama had not understood Papa's dream while Papa lived. So set was she in Old Country ways, she had not even tried to learn to speak English. From now on, Mama would not help Papa who was dead. She would help Mr. Check, who was alive.

"Do you suppose Mr. Truant Officer was married?" Katherine asked wistfully.

Although a year had passed, the stranger had not been forgotten. Otto hiccoughed the last of his tears. He sat up, hiding his face so Katherine could not see his red eyes and tear streaks. He said, "He . . . he didn't say so."

"I must go help Mama," Katherine said. Abruptly she

stood up. Both hands rubbed down her skirt as if she shed one garment to put on another. She left the room.

Once, while Papa was alive, the Meyer children had been taken to an amusement park. Mama scolded about the nickels and dimes Papa spent for their "rides." This did not dim their pleasure in the merry-go-round. They clung to the reins of the wooden horses. They galloped in circles while the calliope shrilled. To Otto, the days that followed Mr. Check's letter seemed the wildest kind of a merry-go-round ride. The Meyers rode in dizzying circles. They always returned to the starting point: They must reach far-off Idaho by September 4.

Mama did not go back to the cannery. Her boss brought her small wages. Otto no longer went out of the neighborhood to look for work. There was much to do at home. The days flew.

Mama knew nothing about cashing money orders, nor did Otto. Vito Rubino went with them to the branch post office. Mama came home with more money than she had ever carried in her purse. At night she hid the money under her mattress; in the daytime she laced it inside her corset. Even then she patted herself dozens of times each day to be sure she had not lost Mr. Check's money.

Otto did not realize the full extent of Mama's ignorance about paper money until he went with her to the railway station, to buy their tickets. Carefully he explained how many Meyers were going to Idaho. He answered the questions about age that applied to rates the ticket agent called "half-fare."

'Board!

"Mama, he means it doesn't cost as much for Hans to travel as it costs for you," Otto explained. The agent checked his schedule and price list and announced the cost.

Mama turned her back to the ticket agent's window. Reluctantly she brought out one bill, a one or five or a ten, for each member of the family. These she pushed through the window. She waited for tickets.

"Not enough, Mama," Otto said.

Again Mama pushed bills. Instead of six bills, she gave five. "Because of Hans," she said thriftily.

"Not enough, Mama," Otto said again. The ticket agent coughed and Otto flushed. He pleaded, "Give me your purse, Mama."

With a suspicious look at the agent, Mama handed Otto her worn purse. She moaned in German as she saw her precious money disappear. "No, no, too much!"

"It costs money to travel, and Idaho is a long way," Otto told Mama. It embarrassed him that he must speak German in this public place. People in the depot paused to listen and watch. Otto was glad to receive the roll of perforated tickets and to escape to the street.

From early morning until midnight Mama washed, ironed and mended clothing and bedding. She laid the articles flat in the trunk Papa had brought from Germany. Among the folds she placed a few odd pieces of Old Country china, the big Bible and her album of photographs. Except for Papa's rocking chair, Big Mike owned the battered furniture. Vito crated the chair for shipment. He gave Mama a packing case. The mattresses were promised to the Rubinos.

On the day before their departure, Katherine discovered she had not returned her library books. "We've read lots of books. We should say thank you," she told her brothers. They agreed. With hair newly cut by the tailor, Israel Fishbein, the four Meyer boys went with Katherine to the library.

Gravely the whisper-voiced librarian accepted their "thank yous." She asked Otto, "Will you live near a library?"

"I don't know," Otto confessed.

"We have some books with ragged covers," she said. "I'd like to give them to you." She led the way to the back room and picked out a dozen books. She told Otto, "For your Papa's ladder."

Mama threw up her hands when the children brought home more books than they had taken away.

"We'll put them in the crate with Papa's rocking chair," Otto promised hastily.

A little group of neighbors went with the Meyers to the station. They waited in the gray pre-dawn for the arrival of the train. Otto heard the shout, " 'Board!" A jumble of good-byes in several languages mixed with the hugs and backslaps.

Maria Rubino gave Otto a grocery carton filled with food. Big Mike added a salami and a string of weiners. Tom-the-printer supplied the children with paper cuttings and stubs of colored pencils.

He explained, "You can amuse yourselves, drawing pictures and playing games."

'Board!

Even Pastor Schmidt arrived at the station in time to pronounce a benediction and mark the air with a cross. Otto thought it odd that the pastor did not seem surprised or upset about their going to Idaho.

Silently self-conscious from all the newness of this experience, Mama, Katherine, Martin, Gussie, Hans and Otto walked away from their neighbors. They crowded into two facing seats of the railroad car. They sat down, knees bumping, toes touching. Otto thought the hour was sunrise, but he was not sure. The sky was black with the smoke of steel mills and oil refineries.

They were leaving the old, facing the new, but they could not point at the passing scene and ask, "Do you remember?" Only Mama had been outside the city limits of Pittsburgh. She did not share her memories.

8

Hiya, Bill

The Meyers had left Pittsburgh in the dim light of early morning. A week later they arrived at Grangeville, Idaho, at midnight, September 4, 1922. Tired, dirty, confused and lost, the sleepy children huddled around Mama, herself a frightened child in a strange place. Hans cried noisily when Otto left for the baggage room.

Otto's business was soon handled. No other passengers had left the train. Only three pieces of luggage must be claimed—Papa's rocking chair, the trunk, and the large wooden box.

Before returning to Mama, Otto stood beside Papa's rocking chair. He waited for Papa's warm closeness to build his courage. Nothing happened. Papa remained in some far place, and Otto stood alone.

Within minutes he would give up his place as "man of the family" to a stranger. He had not been able to change Mama's mind. Otto had no choice. He must find Mr. Check.

Angered by his own helplessness, Otto kicked the utensil box. Then he turned towards the dimly lighted waiting room. His legs were wooden pegs with rusty hinges for knees, but his heart was a living, aching thing.

Otto stopped abruptly when he saw a man approach Mama. They shook hands and stood apart, a tall man and Mama, with a scarf on her head.

So that was Mr. Check. Mr. Bela Karl Czek. Loose-jointed, wearing dark trousers, a plaid shirt and a large hat. Since entering prairie and mountain country, Otto had seen men who wore similar clothing. But . . . there was something about that hat . . .

Hans had been crying dismally, continuously. Suddenly he stopped. At the same time Katherine said, very distinctly, "Why, you're Mr. Truant Officer."

"No," the man answered. "I'm Bela Czek."

Otto strode across the waiting room. Clenching his fists he looked up into the tall man's face. He accused hotly, "You lied to me! You spied on us!"

"I figured you'd think that, Otto," Mr. Check said soberly. "If you will do some recalling, you will realize that *you* said I was a truant officer. I didn't."

Otto gulped. He turned his back on the man and dug his fingers into the depths of his pockets. The man was right. It was he who had jumped to that conclusion, but Mr. Check had allowed it.

By losing his temper Otto sensed that he had upset his brothers and sister. Obviously they were glad to find their dream-maker instead of a total stranger at the end of their long journey. Otto had used up the last of childhood's easy tears on the day Mama received Mr. Check's letter. Now he could only stand and hurt.

At that moment Otto felt stripped of all he held dear —Papa, Mama, the younger children, voices he knew and streets he could walk in the dark.

He could not bear total loss. At no matter what cost to himself, he must recover a place in the family, if not as "man of the family," then as "big brother."

While he struggled with his temper, Otto thought of the summer day Mama had come home late from work. She had mentioned speaking with an old friend. She had said "him."

With aching insight, Otto realized that Mama had placed her problems in Bela Czek's hands months ago. Of course she was not surprised to receive Christmas gifts!

Only Mr. Truant Officer and the whisper-voiced librarian had known about Papa's ladder. That meant Mr. Check had written the note in the Christmas book.

As for the mysterious gifts of money, had Mama lied when questioned about the coal? No, Otto decided. Mama did not understand money. She earned wages. She spent her wages for her children's needs. Otto told himself, "She did not know her wages were too small to support us." Bela Czek had more than made up the difference between income and outgo. He had provided the small extras that added excitement to a hard year. At the same time he had not lessened either Mama's or Otto's own pride in providing for the family. Gratitude caused tears to spring to Otto's eyes. Shock clenched his fists.

"Pastor," Otto thought. "He shopped for Mr. Check. Yes. That's the way it had to have been to make sense. That explained the pastor's "honorable and generous man." Mr. Check must have told Pastor Schmidt the whole story. That explained Pastor's calmness at the station when he marked the air with a cross, blessing this journey.

Standing apart from his family, Otto fought a silent battle with himself, honest enough to recognize Bela Czek's kindness, but young enough to be hurt by the double role the man had played.

"I owe Mr. Check for our food," Otto thought. And for coal, clothing, gifts. Even for the chance to stay in school!

Undersized and young though he was, Otto had courage. It took courage, all he had, to face the group——Mama, Katherine, Martin, Gussie, Hans and Mr. Check. Otto held out his hand. He said stiffly, "I'm sorry I lost my temper. Thank you, sir, for everything."

Mama looked puzzled. So did Katherine, Gussie, Martin and Hans. But Mr. Check understood. Instantly his big hand closed on Otto's thin palm.

"I had it coming," he said, then added soberly, "you're welcome, Otto."

Of the five Meyer children, it was Gussie who needed physical closeness to people. He moved near enough to Mr. Check to touch the dark woolen fabric of his clothing. Katherine rubbed her sides with her palms, in the way she had when faced with change. Martin smiled uncertainly, first at Otto, then at Mr. Check. Mama fussed with the scarf on her blond braids.

79

Hans yawned widely. Suddenly interest lighted his round blue eyes. He invited, "Take me to your river."

"Tomorrow," Mr. Check promised.

"Is there a mountain?" Martin asked wistfully.

"There's a mountain," Mr. Check said. He picked up Hans and the suitcase Mama had kept in the passenger car. He said, "Now I'll take you to your rooms."

The Meyers spent the rest of the night in a plainly furnished hotel room. In the morning, when Otto and Katherine ventured beyond the narrow corridor, they found Mr. Check waiting for them. He asked, "Did you sleep well?"

Gratefully Katherine answered, "There was room to stretch out. It was hard to sleep sitting up in the train seats."

Almost at once they were joined by the younger boys, Martin, Gussie and Hans. Mama was last to appear. Otto saw that Mama had take much pain with the braiding of her blond hair. She had put on a clean white blouse. She looked at Mr. Check's right ear, left ear, chin or hair, but never directly into his gray eyes. Nervously she twisted her wide gold wedding ring.

Mr. Check ordered breakfast at the hotel. Conversation around the big table was a German-English hodgepodge. Though Mama permitted no English spoken in her presence, the children found no way to avoid answering Bela Czek in English. That was the language he used with them. To Mama they spoke German. Otto noticed that only English was spoken by waitresses and other customers.

A dark-skinned man marched to a table and sat down. Martin whispered a question. Mr. Check said briefly, "He's Indian."

Mama seemed to shrink in size. Nervously she watched the Indian drink his coffee.

After breakfast the Meyers huddled around Mama while Mr. Check paid their bill. The man turned at the desk for a long look at the family. Then he picked up Mama's suitcase and walked toward them, putting his feet down firmly, as if he knew exactly where he was going.

"Are you ready, Anna?" he asked when he reached Mama.

Mama did not speak, but she nodded.

Silently the children followed Mr. Check and Mama past some store fronts. They went through a door marked "Justice of the Peace."

A gray-haired man with a moustache rose from behind a big cluttered desk. He held out a hand as he said, "Hiya, Bill. I see your family got here okay."

The men shook hands. Mr. Check introduced Mama as "Mrs. Johann Meyer, the bride-to-be." He pulled a folded paper from his pocket and gave it to the Justice of the Peace.

The Justice asked, "You kids want to stand behind your mama? This won't take long."

Otto gulped and shuffled his feet. Fingers touched his, and he clasped hands with Katherine. She held Gussie's hand, too, so Otto reached for Martin's. Hans refused to hold Martin's hand. He stood beside Mr. Check.

"That's right, son," the Justice said, winking at Hans. "We need a best man at this ceremony."

The Justice called his wife and a clerk for witnesses. He recited the marriage ceremony. When Mr. Check pulled a ring from his pocket and lifted Mama's left hand, there was an awkward pause. Papa's gold band shone brightly on her ring finger.

The Justice said, "Ahem!" He coughed behind his hand. The Justice's wife fanned herself. The clerk looked embarrassed.

Then Mr. Check spoke gently, in German, so that only Mama and the children could understand his words. He asked, "Anna, may I wear Johann's ring? I would feel honored."

For the first time Mama looked straight into Mr. Check's eyes. Slowly she pulled off Papa's gold band. She accepted the ring Mr. Check offered. Papa's ring would not slide over Mr. Check's big knuckle. He put it on the little finger of his left hand.

The Justice said, "You may kiss your bride, Mr. Check."

Otto squeezed Katherine's hand so hard she wriggled, tugged and whispered, "Otto, you're hurting me."

To Otto's relief, Mr. Check did not kiss Mama. He shook hands, clicking his heels and bowing from the hips in the Old Country way. Before he released Mama's work-reddened hand, he raised it to his lips. He kissed the finger that now wore his gold ring.

Mama's lips almost smiled. Nervously she pulled her hand from his and put it behind her back. Only then did Otto's fingers relax their hold on Katherine's jerking hand.

"Mr. and Mrs. Check and all the little Checks," the

Justice said heartily. He shook hands all around and clapped Mr. Check's shoulder. The tall stranger, who was a stranger no longer, but a substitute father, ushered the Meyer family into the street.

Mr. Check pointed away from the center of town. He said, "We walk this way."

For the first time, Otto looked at this wide, high space where he found himself. Forested mountains surrounded a valley. On the horizon loomed a mountain chain so jagged as to look artificial.

"I don't see a river," Hans said.

"You will, Hans," Mr. Check promised.

At the livery stable Mr. Check helped Mama into the high seat of a wagon. Then he lifted the children. Otto stepped onto a wheel hub and boosted himself into the wagon bed. He saw that Mr. Check had already brought Papa's rocking chair, the trunk and wooden box from the railway depot. He added the suitcase, then folded blankets on the big box to make a seat. He advised, "Make yourselves comfortable. We have a long way to go. If you get hungry, you'll find food in that basket."

"T-thank you," Katherine stammered, then added, "s-sir."

"You're welcome, Katherine," Mr. Check said gravely.

When the wagon began to roll Gussie said, "He called you Katherine."

"That's my name," Katherine said.

"But Papas are supposed to call you Katrinka," Gussie said.

"That's my real-Papa name," Katherine explained. Her

lower lip trembled. She clamped it with her teeth.

Puzzled, Gussie asked, "Isn't Mr. Truant Officer our real papa now?"

"Aw, shut up, Gussie!" Otto flared.

Rudeness had never been tolerated in the Meyer house. Gussie stared at Otto with hurt amazement. Then he turned his attention to the road that twisted up, up and up from the valley floor. "It's . . . big . . . out here," Gussie offered, trying to make peace with Otto.

"Yeah," Otto agreed.

9

There's My River

Several hours later Mr. Check cooled his horses at the top of a mountain. An involuntary gasp burst from Otto's rounded lips. He looked out and down, and there seemed to be no end to either dimension.

Mama hunched on the wagon seat and hugged herself. Martin and Gussie clutched the rim of the wagon bed. They stared wordlessly. Hans looked surprised, then one fat finger began to jab air.

"What are you doing, Hansel?" Gussie asked.

"I'm counting," Hans said.

"I didn't know there were so many mountains in the whole world," Martin whispered.

Softly Katherine said, "I wonder if this is the mountain where Satan took Jesus to show Him the world."

Mr. Check turned his head to face Katherine. He, too, looked into the gorge, so wide and deep as to stagger the imagination. He said, "That's very good, Katherine. He'd have been tempted to choose the Whitebird country."

"Where's your river?" Hans asked. He scrambled over the back of the wagon seat to squeeze his sturdy body between Mama and Mr. Check. Hans leaned forward, looking through his blond lashes, prepared to "spot" the river the instant the man pointed.

Mr. Check pointed, but Hans gave up. There were too many mountains, too many creeks, too many canyons, too many rocks and crags and buttes to pinpoint one place in the broad scene. Hans twisted to look into Otto's face. He asked, "Do you see the river, Otto?"

"No, Hans," Otto admitted, "but it must be there . . ."

Under the brim of the big western hat, black-lashed gray eyes examined Otto's face. Smile crinkles formed at lip and eye corners. Otto flushed, knowing this man had read into his words more than he had meant to confess; that his dream of the stranger's mountain was bigger than his jealousy.

"It's there, son," the man said.

Down, down and down again inched the powerful horses, holding back instead of pulling the wagon. Mr. Check braked wheels. On two of the sharpest curves with the deepest dropoffs he walked beside his horses, talking in a soft voice. Once a wheel slipped. He yelled, not in anger, but with mighty authority. The horses responded. Danger was averted.

Ten hours from the time the Meyers climbed into the wagon, they rolled into a village on the banks of a tree-lined creek. "Whitebird," Mr. Check said. "We'll stay here tonight."

Mama, Katherine and Hans slept in a room provided by one of Mr. Check's friends. Otto, Martin and Gussie slept with Mr. Check in the wagon bed.

Tightly rolled in blankets, Otto looked up at a velvet sky

so filled with stars, the shimmer added light to that of the new moon. No industrial smoke, no bawling barges, no rattling coal cars, no scream of siren or blast of whistle disturbed his rest. Still, Otto did not sleep. He could hear the gurgle of water over rocks, the grinding teeth of horses feeding on well-earned oats, the snick-click of a dislodged stone, the rush of wind. Once he heard a wild, garbled cry. He sat up, clutching his blankets.

"Coyotes," Mr. Check said, chuckling in the dark.

"Kind of wild dogs," Martin told Gussie. "Remember, we read about them in the library book."

"Oh. Yes," Gussie said.

Realizing that the younger boys listened and watched, too, Otto fumbled for Gussie's hand. Often Gussie found the nights lonesome. Soon Gussie's fingers relaxed. Otto knew his small brother slept. Then he heard Mr. Check's deep, even breathing. As Otto had comforted Gussie, so Otto felt comforted by the presence of the man.

Mr. Check's friends, the Wilsons, provided a big breakfast for the travelers. Mrs. Wilson heaped plates with pink fried ham, hashed potatoes, biscuits and jam. At each plate stood a tall glass of milk. Hesitantly Otto fingered the bottom of his glass.

"Drink it, son," Mrs. Wilson urged. She brought a huge pitcher of milk and placed it in the middle of the table. "This is cow country. If there's one thing we have plenty of, it's milk."

Otto was used to black coffee. Fresh milk was a rare treat.

Mama pointed at the jam in the dish. Obediently Otto asked Mrs. Wilson what it was.

"Huckleberries," Mrs. Wilson said cheerfully. "They grow in the mountains hereabouts. Say!" She braced hands on hips and examined Mama with undisguised surprise. "Don't you speak English, honey? Sure as shootin', you're gonna have a hard time makin' yourself understood in these parts if you don't learn to talk our lingo."

Otto did not want to hurt Mama. He did not interpret. He knew Mama had sensed the woman's frank criticism. Mama's cheeks reddened. She did not taste the jam, though she looked often at the jam dish.

When Otto pushed back his plate he was careful to leave half a biscuit, well buttered and covered with huckleberry jam. Never a bite of food was allowed to waste in the Meyer house. As he had planned, Mama lifted the biscuit scrap from his plate and ate every crumb.

Otto became aware of Mr. Check's eyes. The man had seen the little drama of the biscuit and jam. He smiled, but his eyes looked stern, too. Mrs. Wilson bustled to the big woodstove to bring the coffeepot. Mr. Check said in a low voice, "Otto, you spoil Mama. You treat her like a child."

"But . . ." Otto argued. He did not finish his sentence. Mrs. Wilson returned to the table. She poured strong, black coffee into Mama's cup.

Night-damp still clung to the leaves and grass when Mr. Check hitched the brown horses to the wagon tongue. He helped Mama to her place in the high wagon seat. He pretended not to notice Hans, then scooped him up to sit

beside Mama. Hans laughed aloud. The older children climbed into the wagon bed.

"Giddap!" Mr. Check shouted. Again the wheels began to roll. Almost at once they reached the bank of a broad river. Proudly, Mr. Check said, "There it is, Hans. There's my river."

Otto saw a wide and pleasant river, clean-bottomed and lined with stretches of sand and gravel bars. Trees cast green reflections. Foothills rolled up from the edge of the valley. Beyond the foothills loomed the jagged mountains.

"It's green," Hans said with deep satisfaction. Hans was prepared to accept this river. He understood green. There

had been so little of it in the slums of Pittsburgh; even a dandelion's green leaves made an impression.

Martin asked, "What's the river's name?"

"This is the Salmon," Mr. Check said.

"No one chose the Salmon," Katherine said. "It didn't look big on the map."

"But it is," Hans said. Life was going exactly as he liked to have it go. His river was green and it was big. He was well fed and he sat between a mother and a father again. He was soberly happy in a typically Hans way.

They crossed the Salmon river. A right turn led downriver from Whitebird creek and the village of Whitebird, back into the foothills of the fabulous mountains.

While he drove, Mr. Check talked. He told of fur traders, Indian battles, prospectors and cattlemen who had lived and died in the gorge. Once in a while he spoke in German, but most of the time his words were in English.

Otto noticed this. He asked accusingly, "Why did you write your letter in German?"

"It was to Anna, your mama," the man answered with dignity.

"Then why are you leaving her out now?" Otto asked coldly.

"I . . ." Apologetically the man looked at Mama. "It's been so long since I've spoken German — I forget," he explained.

A silence developed.

Katherine squirmed on the utensil box. Then she said, "We thought you were a miner."

"I was, but I got caught in a cave-in. Cracked my skull. Kind of lost my taste for mines." Mr. Check fingered the scar with its fringe of white hair. "That's when I decided to homestead in Idaho."

Mr. Check told about those days. To save money he "rode the rails" from Colorado, but got caught and had to buy a railroad ticket. In the Salmon river country he figured he had been "taken" by a locator who sold him land thirty-five miles off the road. He built a sod house, bought absolute necessities and began to clear his land.

Other settlers gave up. The only reason Bill Check stayed was because one of his horses had gone over a cliff in an accident. He had no way to pull a wagon from the gorge. As neighbors passed his house, they yelled, "Hey, Check! I left a couple of sheep over at my place!" — or a cow, or a steer, or maybe chickens. He could not bear the thought of all those neglected animals going hungry. He rounded them up and brought them home. He tried to take care of them.

"Believe me," he said with a rueful chuckle, "for a year or two neither my stock nor I got fat."

He told Mama, "After a while the rains came. Now my herds are growing and," he finished quietly, "so is my family."

Timidly Mama asked, "Have you been lonely, Bela Karl?"

"Yes," Mr. Check admitted, "but I've had a good life. I've read a lot. I had a pretty good education in Hungary. I didn't find it hard to learn to speak and read English." He chuckled and added, "If you call our western speech English."

"I like the way you talk," Gussie said earnestly. He grinned shyly when Mr. Check winked at him.

The horses clop-clopped. Martin and Gussie dozed. Otto and Katherine spoke only occasionally. A pointing finger was enough to indicate the object that drew attention — a hawk, cattle on a ridge, or a prospector panning for gold.

"By the way," Mr. Check said, after a long silence, "my name is not Bela Czek. When I filed for citizenship I changed my name to Bill Check."

"Bill," Katherine repeated. She nodded approval.

The younger boys were awake now. Martin asked hesitantly, "What are we supposed to call you?"

"Papa," Hans said at once.

Otto gasped and glared at Hans.

Mr. Check noticed. He said, "Call me Bill. Everyone else does."

"Is it polite to call a mister Bill?" Gussie whispered so loudly even Mr. Check overheard and laughed.

"It is," Mr. Check said, "when I give you permission."

"Bill. Mr. Check," Otto thought. Into his head popped the words, "my stepfather, Bill Check." He stopped that thought before it grew. He was not ready for a father-son relationship.

In Pittsburgh, Otto had worked for any man who gave him the chance to earn money for his family. Otto was prepared to work for this man, Bill Check, but he was prepared to move cautiously. Bill Check lived life on his own terms. Bill asked no favors. It was he who gave the permission. He left no room for doubt. He was head of the house of Check, and now the Meyers were Checks.

10

Ride Like a Native Son

That day in Pittsburgh when Mr. Truant Officer had leaned on the stone wall to look down on the old "Mon," Otto had been unable to picture the space the man talked about. Now, with the space above, around and even below, Otto hunched his shoulders. He felt his own smallness.

Hans did not hunch. He held the reins of the brown horses. He learned to click his tongue when Bill told him that sound urged the horses to go faster. " 'Cause we want to get home," Hans explained to Gussie and Martin. They leaned on the back of the wagon seat. They waited for a turn in the driver's seat.

Otto did not ask to drive. Though Bill did not offer the reins to Otto, he gave his instructions in a voice loud enough to reach both Katherine and Otto in the wagon bed.

After leaving the village of Whitebird, Otto saw that no more than a half-dozen roads branched from the downriver route. Only once did he see a roof. A smudge of smoke indicated a chimney.

"Andersons proved up on this claim," Bill said. Much later he pointed at a backbone of rock on the skyline.

"Tippitts live up on the ridge," he said. "They're our neighbors."

Martin was "driving" when they passed close to the base of a great rockslide. He said, "A giant must have pounded that mountain to pieces."

"That's just what happened," Bill agreed. "The giant was water, wind and time." He took the reins from Martin's fingers and turned the horses up a steep bank. They went through an almost hidden stone archway and into a broad, grassy valley. Bill said, "Home."

Hans pushed between Martin and Bill. He stood beside Bill's knees to survey the valley where log buildings sat firmly on riverstone foundations. Hans said, "There's the river. It's green."

"And the mountain," Martin said.

Gussie scolded, "You can't count, Martin. There are lots of mountains."

"Wheresa mule deer, an' I don't remember what it is?" Hans asked all in one breath.

"Take a squint at that haystack and you'll see one," Bill said. "That's a big fellow. I'd say he's a two-hundred pounder."

Otto rose from the utensil box. He shaded his eyes. At first he saw only cows and their calves in the sloping meadow. Then he saw flicking white ears, a light throat patch and a rack of antlers. Breathlessly Otto asked, "Does he come here often?"

Dryly Bill answered, "Sure. He knows a good thing when

he finds it. There is good browse in that meadow and nothing to fear."

Home. Nothing to fear. Those were the words that stuck in Otto's mind like burrs in wool while Bill Check drove through the meadow. The wagon stopped beside a wide porch.

Dropping reins, Bill said, "This is where we live." He reached across the space in front of Martin's chest. He tilted Mama's chin with gentle fingertips. Bill said softly, speaking in German, "Anna, this is your home for the rest of your life."

Mama murmured but no words came out. She had been silent during yesterday's descent into the gorge. She had said very little during today's downriver drive. Most of the time she hugged herself into as small a space as possible. She darted quick glances right and left.

Otto thought, "Mama is afraid." Mama had been afraid in Pittsburgh, too. Only inside four walls with the people she knew and loved did Mama feel secure.

Katherine was first to climb down from the wagon. She walked to a kitchen window. Shading eyes with both hands, she pushed her face against the glass.

"Go on in, Katherine," Bill invited. "The door isn't locked."

"Not locked?" Mama gasped. "Would you have yourself robbed of the food on your shelves, the blankets on your bed?"

Bill smiled at Mama's outburst. "Everything is safe. You'll

see." With a little chuckle he added, "Who is around to take things?"

Who, indeed, Otto thought, with a swift glance at the mountains. They built a great wall against the skyline on three sides. The wide, swift river protected the fourth.

Bill unloaded the trunk, Papa's rocking chair, the utensil box and suitcase. He lined them up on the wide porch that faced the river. He told Mama, "We'll take things in when you decide where to put them."

Proudly Bill led his new family into this house he had built with his own hands. Otto liked the large living room. Its windows were placed to let in sunlight and view. Most of the furniture had been built of peeled logs and rawhide. The chairs were upholstered with leather. When Bill saw Otto trace an odd brown design with his fingertips, he explained, "The leather is cowhide, and that's my cattle brand."

Otto saw that there would be space for the books given by the whisper-voiced librarian. Bill would not throw up his hands as Mama had done. His own books, much read, stood on long shelves.

"Clean," Mama said, tapping the well-oiled floor.

Otto had never seen such a kitchen. The table was large enough to seat a dozen people, with plenty of elbow room. Benches stood around the table, seats planed to satin smoothness. The children sat on the benches. They tapped their feet on the floor to test the height.

Mama walked to the large wood range. She worked dampers and lifted lids. Hesitantly she examined a wooden trough lined with metal. She turned a tap and asked in wonder, "The water, where does it come from?"

"From a spring up on the hill," Bill told her. To Otto he said, "Gravity flow." Gussie and Martin looked impressed when Otto nodded his head.

Bill opened the kitchen door and led the way into a hall. The floor was so new no bootmarks scarred the wood. Three bedrooms lay beyond the hall. One held a large bed with shiny brass balls on its four posts; the second, two sets of bunks. A cot with a white bedspread stood in the third. Soberly Bill said, "For you, Katherine."

"It's . . . new," Katherine said breathlessly. "When . . .?"

"After meeting you, I had a year to build this ell," Bill said.

Softly and earnestly Katherine said, "You wanted us."

"More than I've ever wanted anything," Bill answered. "The years are long when you live alone."

After inspecting the house, the whole family walked between a row of young fruit trees to the barn and sheds. The boys worked with eager clumsiness when Bill showed them how to feed the livestock in the corral.

"This will take a while," Bill told Mama. "Maybe you'd like to get supper started, Anna. Just open the cupboard. You'll find supplies."

Obedient as a child, Mama returned to the house to prepare this first meal in her new home. When Bill and the boys returned from the barn, she gave them thin potato soup, a small pan of biscuits, and black coffee.

Bill looked at the meager meal. Silently he lifted his

spoon. He did not criticize Mama's effort. But when the meal was finished he said gently, "There's lots of meat, milk, butter, eggs. If there is one thing we ranchers do well, it is to eat."

Mama fluttered her hands. "But there are so many of us. We do not wish to impose. We are so grateful . . ." The German words rolled awkwardly from her tongue while she tried to explain her position in this house.

"Grateful!" Bill exploded. He stood up and placed both hands on Mama's shrinking shoulders. He shook her, as a pup shakes a toy. Firmly he said, "Get this through your head, Anna Check. This is your name, for better, for worse. Your children are my children, for better, for worse. You take care of me and the kids and the house, and let me worry about earning a living. Do you understand?" With a final shake of Mama's shoulders, Bill stood away from her. Gray eyes glowed with the intensity of his emotion.

Otto looked at Bill's big hands, aware of their strength. He listened to the big voice that spoke with such authority. That he, Otto Meyer, was no longer "man of the family," Otto did not doubt. At that moment he would not have cared to argue the point.

During their first week on the ranch the Meyer children tiptoed inside the house. They went always in pairs when they left the porch. They shrank from contact with the animals till Bill showed them how to rub down and curry the horses. They had never owned a dog or a cat. They loved the horses.

With much effort Otto learned to draw a dribble of milk

from a patient cow. Martin began to conquer nervousness. He no longer ran from the chickens when they crowded about him, clucking, lifting wings.

Bill did not laugh at Martin. He explained, "They don't want to peck you, Martin. They want to see if there is food in that bucket."

When the weekend came, Bill said, "Your holiday is over. Monday you'll go to school."

Amazed that school was held in the gorge, Katherine asked, "Where?"

"I'll take you the first time," Bill promised. "You'll have to ride horseback. Think you'd better practice?"

"Oh, boy," Hans crowed.

"Not you, silly," Gussie scoffed. "You don't go to school."

"Well, I can practice for when I do go," Hans argued. Gussie. was not convinced. Hans appealed to Bill, "Can't I, Papa?"

Each time Hans said "Papa," the man's lashes fluttered. Bill licked his lips before answering. When he spoke, his voice was gentle. He agreed, "Certainly, son. Next year when you start to school, you'll ride like a native son."

"Whatsa . . ." Hans began.

Bill slapped Hans' shoulder and urged, "Come on. We have to put a halter on one of those four-legged hay burners."

Otto walked a little apart, listening, watching. When with the children, Bill did not speak German. Otto wished Mama understood English, for in the German language Bill's easygoing western speech was lost. His voice kept its

101

Hungarian music, but slowed to the tempo of flowing river, grasses bending in wind, and the thud of hooves. This Otto could not interpret for Mama. He could only listen, with a sense of wonder that this man had merged so completely with the American scene in thirteen years.

It was different with Papa. Papa had remained German, with much enthusiasm for things American. Bill Check *was* American. Papa's dream was for the future. Bill Check lived his life here and now.

When Bill lifted Hans to the back of the big brown horse, then walked beside him, Otto felt a little rush of warmth that was almost love. Quickly he stifled the emotion as something disloyal to Papa. He sat alone on a corral rail while Papa's big watch ticked inside his pocket.

The younger children rode in endless slow circles. When his own turn came, Otto followed instructions, but he did not look at Bill.

Gussie asked, "Don't you like to ride, Otto?"

"Sure," Otto replied.

Gussie shrugged. He said frankly, "You don't look it."

Otto snapped, "What do you know about how I'm supposed to look?"

"Well," Gussie said judiciously, "I know you don't look like Papa. He . . ."

Fiercely Otto shouted down at Gussie, "Papa was never on a horse!"

"He . . ." Gussie began, red-faced with anger to match's Otto's. Then the small boy seemed to shrink. Uncertainly he looked from Otto on the back of the brown horse to Bill

Check. Bill walked beside Martin's horse at the far end of the corral. In a dead voice Gussie said, "Oh. You mean that other Papa we used to have."

"I mean our *real* Papa," Otto argued. He felt deeply guilty for the confusion he was causing Gussie, but he was unable to keep quiet, so confused was he himself.

"Just who *do* you mean?" Gussie asked. He pointed at Bill. "This Papa is *real*. And that other Papa . . ." Gussie looked up at the wide western sky. "I don't know about that other Papa," the small boy admitted. "He isn't here."

Nor did Otto know about that other Papa. He was not here, even in the night when Otto tried to bring him close, by recalling the things he had said, the things he had done, the way he had laughed, the way he had scowled, the clothes he had worn, the food he had eaten.

When Otto tried hardest to remember Papa, Bill Check's living personality got in the way. It was not easy to keep two fathers.

11

Come Stop Mama

Hans shared the excitement of the first ride to the country school. He clung to Bill Check's saddle horn and shouted to Gussie, "I'm sitting in Papa's lap!"

The easy swing of Bill's shoulders as he sat astride his spotted Appaloosa reassured Otto. Had he remained in Pittsburgh, he would be working at odd jobs or in one of Mr. Heinz's pickle factories, while Katherine, Martin and Gussie went to school. But here he was, astride a tall horse on the stranger's mountain, just as he had dreamed. He owed much to Bill Check, but it was a debt Otto was not ready to pay.

The trail led up and out of the hidden valley behind the stone arch. At each turn of the trail, new color, distance and depth were revealed.

Long before they came to the school, Otto caught sight of the small, square building. A corral and a shed lay at one side. At the foot of a steep rock cliff the Salmon river gnawed the roots of mountains.

"At this place," Otto thought, "we will start to climb up Papa's ladder;" that ladder the whisper-voiced librarian said reached from the place where they were to the place Papa wanted them to be. Papa had dreamed of helping his children to climb out of poverty. He had believed knowledge to be the first rung on the ladder. Although they had never talked about it, Otto was sure Bill Check shared this belief. After all, he had written in the flyleaf of the Christmas book, "Knowledge will help you climb the ladder." Bill had lifted a whole family out of the slums, and now he was taking that same family to school. Yes, Otto thought. Bill might never talk about it, but he dreamed of ladders, too.

Several horses stood in the corral when the Meyers arrived. Bill helped his children care for their saddles and feedbags. He jerked a thumb at a freckled, lanky boy who pumped water into a wooden trough. "If you need help, whistle for Ed Tippitt. He was born on a horse."

Hearing his name, the lanky boy came forward. He said, "So you're Bill's kids." He did not question. He made a statement of fact.

Otto gulped, but Katherine spoke for her brothers. "Yes, Bill Check is our new father."

Bill introduced the Meyers to a middle-aged woman with alert brown eyes. With Hans, he then headed back over the home trail.

Hans called back, "Papa and I gotta work!"

School was unlike anything Otto had ever experienced. Besides the Meyers, ten pupils in eight grades studied, recited and played together. Four Andersons came from the downriver ranch. Three were Tippitts who lived on the ridge.

One was the son of the Anderson's foreman, and two were the daughters of a prospector who worked a gravel bar for gold.

With a dictionary, a set of maps, encyclopedias and a few extra reference books, the teacher, Mrs. Pringle, created an atmosphere that invited hard work. With her help, to study was to adventure. Otto liked Mrs. Pringle. He felt himself liked in return.

During a lull in the activity, Otto thought, "This is the only teacher I've ever had who did not know Papa." On the heels of the thought came another, "But she knows Bill."

Through the days of that fall, Otto lived with his seesaw thoughts: Papa, Bill, Papa, Bill.

In a shorter time than seemed possible, the Meyer children adjusted to ranch life. Otto kept his position as big brother, but he no longer carried Papa's big watch. He left it in his dresser drawer. He was not the man of the family.

Otto shared Bill's fall work. Together they brought cattle, sheep and horses from the high country to the home corrals. Bill always checked before Otto straddled a horse or picked up a pitchfork. He asked, "Got your homework done, son?" At first that word "son" hit Otto's heart. After a while he accepted the word and would have missed its use.

Martin had never fully regained his health after his operation. Now he grew stronger with the passing of time. Though he was the Meyer most apt to need company, Gussie sometimes chose to be alone.

Hans was Bill's constant companion. Each night at the supper table Hans told about the coyote he had seen, the eagle he had heard, or the calf he had almost roped. The rest of the Meyers said, "You're lucky, Hansel."

Otto saw that Hans was leaving babyhood to become a sturdy, capable boy. Once Otto heard Mama scold cheerfully, "Hansel, you're just like your papa." Hans was like Bill, not like Johann Meyer. Hans was becoming the son Bill Check had never had.

Mama seldom left the four walls of the house, even to walk to corrals or sheds. Katherine did the work that was new to Mama's hands. Mama had not fitted into the neighborhood in Pittsburgh. She was not at home on a western ranch. Even Hans knew this about Mama and tried to protect her.

Bill was aware of the children's protection. Often his eyes darkened. Shaking his head, he said nothing. Or if he spoke, it was to say gently, "It is you who should protect your children, Anna."

Once, seeing Mama's blue eyes flood with tears, Otto flared, "How can she? She doesn't know what people are saying! But she was going to do the best she could. In Pittsburgh she got a job in the cannery. You stopped her!"

For a long moment Bill was silent. Then he said, "She came to me willingly, Otto."

"Because of a handshake a long time ago!" Otto shouted.

Almost timidly Mama told Otto, "Bela is right, Otto. I made the choice."

Seldom did Bill touch Mama, or even sit near her. Now

he reached across the space between them and patted
Mama's hand. Mama ducked her head. She did not move
her hand. Some sort of magic quivered in the kitchen,
almost welding a family together. Then Mama put her
hand in her apron pocket. Again they became three
separate people: Bill, Mama, Otto — each feeling slightly
uncomfortable.

On that weekend the Meyers rode with Bill to drive
marketable beefstock up the river road to Whitebird. They
came home with more money than Bill had sent to Mama
for the railroad tickets, more money than Otto had ever
seen in his life.

"This is our winter's food, new shoes for the whole kit
and kaboodle, Christmas, birthday presents, extra hay for
the stock if we happen to have a hard winter, a book or
two, and," Bill winked solemnly at Hans, "maybe even a
bottle of castor oil!"

"Ugh," Hans said.

During the laughter that followed Hans' grunt of distaste,
Bill put his full wallet in a tin can. He set the can on a
shelf. He whistled when he went to the corral.

Otto reached for his jacket, preparing to follow.

Mama followed Otto to the porch. "What did he say?"
she asked, keeping her eyes on the tin can.

"Oh, Mama," Otto began impatiently, only dimly aware
that Bill had spoken in English. "Why don't you . . .?"
Otto bit his tongue on his criticism. He followed Bill, who
was getting ready to slaughter beef for table use and
needed all the help he could get.

109

It was cold now. The earth crackled with frost. Dark came earlier and lasted longer. The children had less time to spend out of doors. Just as he had done in Pittsburgh, Otto worked early and late to help support his family.

"Butchering is messy," Bill said when they washed up in the horse trough. "But it is a mighty big satisfaction to know your family is going to eat well, come snow time." Otto grunted in agreement. He remembered the potatoes he had cleaned for Vito Rubino.

Mama worked, too. She made sausages and head cheese. She scalded, scraped and sudsed to keep her kitchen clean and orderly. Several times she scolded about the wallet in the tin can.

"I'll ride over the mountain to Grangeville to put it in the bank," Bill promised, "first chance I get."

Mama's lips moved, repeating the word she had understood, Grangeville.

Otto and Katherine were doing homework at the big kitchen table. Katherine said, "I do wish Mama would try to learn to speak English. It's such a bother to tell her what her own husband says."

Though Otto frowned at Katherine for daring to criticize Mama, secretly he agreed. Mama should try. Bill had spoken English for so long he did not always remember to speak German for Mama's benefit.

After the butchering, a horse cut by barbed wire took up much of Bill's time. He did not ride to Grangeville as he had planned. Then the first snow came. "I'll wait for a good foundation underfoot. Less apt to break a horse's leg by a

fall on ice," he said. "We don't get much snow in the gorge, but they have real winter up in the Grangeville country."

Bill was in the barn when the peddler came. So were Katherine, Otto, Gussie and Hans. They saw the man with his pack string come through the stone arch. It was pleasant in the barn, with its odor of hay, leather, cows and dust. They stayed where they were until curiosity pulled Gussie into the house. He came back, eyes wide with excitement. He reported, "Mama's buying stuff. Lots and *lots* of stuff!"

Uneasily Otto looked at Bill.

The man grinned. He said cheerfully, "Reckon she's been feeling cooped up. Buying some pretties will cheer her."

Eager to see Mama's purchases, Katherine buttoned her coat. She hurried from the barn to the house. Almost at once she burst through the kitchen door and slipped and slid down the slushy corral path. She shrieked, "Otto! Come here! Come stop Mama!"

Bill frowned, then shrugged. He told Otto, "Better go see what's up."

Otto had been oiling harness. He put down a halter, scrubbed his hands on a rag and went back to the house with Katherine. He stopped to scrape his feet on the doormat before entering the kitchen. The words he heard made him push open the door and plunge into the room.

"Not enough, lady," Otto heard a coaxing voice say. "One more. One more. One more."

Otto saw a heap of small articles on the kitchen table: spices, thread, needles, ribbons, a shiny pie tin, bright pink soap, a big bottle of vanilla. He saw a wad of paper money in the peddler's left hand. His right hand reached for the bill Mama clutched against her chest. Bill's empty wallet lay on the table beside the tin can, and Martin stood behind Mama.

"Mama!" Otto shouted. "What are you doing?"

The peddler was a small man, not much taller than Otto, dark-skinned and unshaven. One of his teeth was broken. The tooth showed when the man snarled, "Come on, lady, pay up!"

With a scared glance from Otto to the peddler, Mama thrust the last bill into the man's hands. She poked the wallet into the tin can and hurried to put the can back on the shelf.

Otto yelled in anger and fright, "Mama, that was a hundred-dollar bill you gave him!" He grabbed the man's arm and shouted, "Give it back!"

The peddler shook him off. He left the house so hastily he did not bother to pick up his pack.

"Bill!" Otto yelled. "Help!" He was too excited to realize that Bill was in the barn and could not hear him.

Mama whirled on Otto. She clamped her hand over his mouth. She ordered, "Hush!"

"But the money!" Otto shouted. "Those were all hundred-dollar bills, Mama! You gave the man all of Bill's money!"

Katherine whirled away from the open door. Mama saw that she was going to the barn. Mama grabbed Katherine's arm. Fiercely she faced her children and ordered, "Otto! Katherine! Martin! You are not going to tell Bela, now or

113

ever!" She breathed deeply, and her voice quavered when she finished with, "Do you want Bela to beat me?"

While the frightened children considered the awful possibility of Mama's receiving a beating, the peddler rode his horse through the meadow. Galloping madly, he was almost to the stone arch when Katherine tried again to go to Bill. This time Mama locked the door. Stonily she told Otto, Martin and Katherine, "You are not to tell. When Bela finds out, he will think the money was stolen by a thief."

"That's cheating Bill!" Katherine said hotly.

Mama refused to listen to argument. Frightened by what she had done, she raced from table to shelf to bedroom, storing or hiding the cheap articles she had purchased at such great cost. Almost hysterically she said, over and over, "Bela must not know. He would beat me. He would send us away. Where would we go? What would we eat?"

Speechless with the enormity of this thing Mama had done and refused to confess, Otto sat on the edge of a kitchen bench. He stared at the puddle spreading from the soles of his wet boots.

Indeed, where would they go? What would they eat?

Katherine argued, "Bill has to know, Mama. He doesn't have a regular job in a mine or a factory. There won't be any more money until the steers get big enough to sell."

"He is not to know!" Mama screamed.

"I'm going to tell!" Katherine screamed right back.

"Otto!" Mama ordered. "*You* are the head of this family! Stop her. Don't let her go to the barn."

"No, Mama," Otto said, swallowing tears. "I am not the

114

head of this family. Bill is." Gently he told Katherine, "Stay with Mama, Katrinka. I will tell Bill."

"Ot — to!" Mama wailed, but Otto did not look back. He could not run down the path. His legs felt almost too weak to carry his weight.

When Otto reached the barn he leaned against the door-jamb. He looked at this man who had willingly accepted the responsibility Mama had unloaded, first on Otto, then on Bela Czek. For the first time, Otto allowed himself to love Bill. "But it's too late," he thought. "Bill will hate Mama for cheating him. He'll send us away." Aloud, he said, "Papa . . ."

Bill's head jerked up. "What . . . did you call me?" he asked.

"Papa . . ." Otto repeated.

In alarm Bill asked, "What is it, son?"

"It's Mama," Otto answered. No other words would come, so he repeated, "It's Mama."

12

Hole in the Ground

When Otto told him what Mama had done, Bill did not go to the house. He saddled his big Appaloosa and set off to catch the thieving peddler. Bill did not return for supper. The children placed themselves at the windows to watch for his return through the stone arch beyond the meadow.

Darkness came. Still Bill did not come home.

Gussie, who needed the closeness of people, pushed against Katherine's side. He whispered, "Trinka, where's Papa?"

Stony-faced with fright for Bill's safety, and anger at Mama's behavior, Katherine told Gussie, "The man had a head start. Maybe Bill had to ride a long way."

Martin reminded, "There's mud on the trail. His horse could slip and . . ."

Otto shivered, knowing what that could mean. Bill could have fallen into the gorge. During the hard days when he was building his ranch, a horse had fallen from a ledge. It could happen again.

Mama did not sit with the children. Alone in the living room, she rocked in Papa's big .chair. Otto could hear the chair rock and the floorboards squeak. He wondered what Mama was thinking.

"I guess this is what happens to all our Papas," Hans said. "They go away, and they don't come back." Tears rolled down his cheeks, but he did not bellow with his mouth open. Hans was no longer a baby.

"He'll . . . come back," Katherine promised shakily.

Hans went to sleep with his head on the window ledge. Gussie hunched in a ball in the corner of the kitchen. Katherine took her younger brothers to bed. She returned to keep Otto company.

It was long past midnight when they heard the familiar thump of the big Appaloosa's hooves on cold earth. Both Otto and Katherine put on their jackets and stumbled to the barn. They found Bill rubbing down the spotted horse's coat.

"Did you find the man, Papa?" Katherine asked.

"No, Trinka," Bill said.

Bill did not invite speech, but Otto and Katherine stayed there. They drew courage from the orderly barn. Shadows stretched away from Bill's lantern. A milk cow moved in her stall. When Bill had fed his horse, he picked up the lantern. He waited for the children to leave the barn. Silently he locked the door and trudged to the house.

The three found Mama in the kitchen. With a blanket around her shoulders she stood in the middle of the floor. Wide and blue as Gussie's, her eyes flooded with tears.

Bill closed the door. He waited for Otto and Katherine to reach the warm circle near the kitchen range. Then he

117

walked towards Mama. With his step forward, Mama stepped backward. She shrank against the wall.

"You — you are going to beat me?" Mama asked piteously.

"Did Johann beat you?" Bill asked.

"No!"

"Maybe he should have," Bill said. "Since he kept you a child, he should have punished you in the same way."

Mama . . . a child? Otto's eyes searched for Katherine's reaction. He saw that his sister agreed with Bill.

"Beat me, beat me!" Mama screamed. "But don't send us away. We have no place to go, no . . ."

Bill interrupted. "I am not sending you away, Anna, and I'll never strike you. You are my wife. This is your home. I will go."

"Go . . .?" Otto burst out.

"I'll get a job till spring," Bill told Otto and Katherine. "Since all I know is ranching and mining, I'll have to find work in a mine."

"What did he say?" Mama asked Katherine.

"Oh, Mama!" Katherine flared. She burst into tears held back during the long, trying night.

Bill put his arm around Katherine's shaking shoulders. He held her against his side while he faced Mama.

"Anna," Bill said in German. "I could not find the thief. I saw the sheriff. Perhaps sometime the money will be recovered. Until it is, we have no money and a long winter lies ahead. I will find a job. You will not suffer — BUT — "

That one word, "but," sounded so final, Otto thought he could hear the thumping of his own heart.

119

"But," Bill went on, "never again are you to be treated like a child. When I am gone from this house, the responsibility is not Otto's, not Katherine's, not Martin's, not Gussie's, not Hans'. It is *yours*. And," Bill said forcefully, "you are going to learn to speak English!"

"I — I can't!" Mama cried.

"You can, and you are going to," Bill ordered. "You are not going to stumble through life grasping a word here, a word there. You are a grown woman, accountable for your own mistakes.

"This time I will excuse you, since I know you did not understand and could not count the money, but never again. I married a woman, not a child!"

Bill glared so fiercely, Mama pulled her blanket over her face. He pulled it down, forcing her to look at him.

"I can't, I can't, I can't!" Mama sobbed.

"Anna, you can," was all Bill said. He guided Katherine into the hall. He told Otto, "Come on, son, it's long past bedtime. We have a lot to do before I leave. I'm afraid you'll have to miss a few days of school while you help me."

Bill turned back to Mama. Gently he said, "Don't be afraid to grow up, Anna. That is why we are born, to grow up and do our share of the world's work."

Bill waited in the hall until Katherine called, "Goodnight, Papa."

Hearing his sister's words, Otto drew a shivering breath and stammered, "G — goodnight, P — Papa."

"Goodnight, Trinka. Goodnight, son," was the quiet, deep-voiced answer.

Several times Otto swallowed while his fingers plucked at the wool ties of his patchwork quilt. Twice tonight he had said, "Papa." Needing a father's strength, he had found it in Bill Check. Did that mean he had forgotten Papa?

With all his power, Otto concentrated, trying to bring Papa into the room. Fleetingly he glimpsed Papa's face and heard his big voice. But the words he remembered were, "Anna, do this —" and "Anna, do that —" as one speaks to a child. Never, "Anna, what do you think?"

It was Papa who had kept Mama from growing up. Papa had studied. He had explored the city. He had not taken Mama with him. He had not even explained his dream. He had talked to the whisper-voiced librarian as one adult talks to another, but he had not talked to Mama.

At last Otto understood why Mama shifted responsibility onto a son's shoulders, why she expected Katherine to do the unfamiliar ranch work, why she expected to be told what people said, why she had married Bill without questioning Papa's decision — yes, and why she was afraid.

Mama was a child-woman.

She did not understand the world and the people in it, and they did not understand Mama. And it was Papa's fault. Papa had dreamed of a ladder for his children but he had not shown Mama the first rung.

"What would have happened to us," Otto wondered, "if Bill hadn't found us?"

Wise, kind Bill — and lucky, lucky Mama to have a husband who understood her. Mama was not going to think herself lucky, not for a long time. Mama would cry; Mama would storm; but Otto did not doubt for a moment that

Mama would learn English. Mama was used to obeying. It would take her a long time to learn to think for herself. Perhaps she would never free herself from dependence, but Bill would see to it that she tried.

Bill.

Papa . . .

Otto felt hot tears slide into his pillow, but he did not make a sound. Somehow, he knew that never again would he be able to pull Papa into the room by the force of vivid memory. Otto had seen Papa through the eyes of his children, his wife, the librarian, but now he saw Papa through Bill Check's eyes, and Papa was less than perfect.

From this night, Papa was not to be worshipped as an idol, but remembered as a man.

In the dark room Otto stepped away from childhood, aching for what had been, but accepting what was to be.

Bill lost no time in putting his plan into action. He found an Indian herder, Saul Whiteclaw, to run the ranch. He talked to Mrs. Pringle and she agreed to teach Mama to speak English.

"You're to go to school with the children on Mondays and Fridays," Bill told Mama. "Otto and Katherine will help you with your homework. When I come home in the spring, you will be talking so fast I won't be able to keep up with you."

Mama smiled weakly. She promised, "I'll try."

Gently Bill said, "That's all I expect from you, Anna."

"We'll help, Papa," Martin promised eagerly, speaking for his brothers and sister.

122

On the day Mama packed Bill's suitcase, she checked each article of clothing to see that buttons were sewed on and socks darned. Bill stood at the window, looking at his valley. One finger rubbed the scar with its fringe of white hair.

Otto noticed and asked, "Have you worked in a mine since you were hurt?"

"No," Bill said. "I didn't expect to go back underground."

"You're doing this for us," Otto said soberly.

Bill turned from the window. He demanded, "Why not? It is a father's privilege to work for his family."

"But . . ." Otto said hesitantly. He kept his eyes on the scar and the white hair. "Does a father have to do something if he's afraid?"

Otto waited, frightened by what he had said, but sensing that Bill dreaded a return to the mine. Vividly, Otto remembered his own rush through the night when he worked for Tom-the-printer.

Bill's expressive face tightened. His eyes flinched as from a blow. Then he said, "Thank you, Otto, for making me face up to something I've been hiding from myself. Yes, I'm afraid; and, yes, I must do it. We wouldn't starve without the money, but I would always feel that I had done less than my share if I didn't go back to the mine. I'm expecting your mother to overcome her fear of life, so I must overcome my fear of a hole in the ground. I can't expect more of any member of my family than I am ready to give."

His gray eyes glowed. "Understand?" Bill asked.

123

"Yes, Papa," Otto said, feeling deep respect for this strong man who dared to admit fear, and whose code included fair play. "I'll help Mama," he promised.

"See that you do," Bill said soberly, "but let the decisions be hers. When I'm away, Anna is head of the Check family. She is my wife. If she makes mistakes, I'll pay for them."

"Yes, sir," Otto said gratefully.

When Bill left the room to help Mama with the packing, Otto knew he had been handed a gift. Bill had lifted the weight from his back. Bill had given Otto his teen years for growing. Papa would have approved.

13

Ach, This English

The first time Saul Whiteclaw sat down to eat with the family, Mama slapped a plate of hot food in front of him. She ran back to the stove. Throughout the meal she managed to hold something heavy in her hand, a butcher knife, the pot of hot coffee, even the lid lifter from the range.

Uneasily Bill asked, "Anna, is something wrong?"

Mama ducked her head. She shook it with vigor, but she did not take her eyes from Saul. He wiggled his shoulders. He looked from Bill to Mama, then at each of the children in turn. The minute his plate was clean, Saul stood up. Bowing with ceremony, he said, "Excuse me." He left the house.

With a shivering breath, Mama put down her butcher knife.

"He won't hurt you," Otto said.

Mama's hands clutched her braid-wrapped head. She said darkly, "I have heard about scalping."

Bill laughed so hard he sputtered in his coffee. He shouted, "Saul? Saul——hurt somebody? Never! Both his father and his grandfather are leaders in Indian affairs.

125

Saul is a law student at the University of Idaho. He's home for a semester to earn money to go back. I couldn't find a better guardian for you and the kids, Anna."

At once the children set about making friends with Saul. Mama did not relax. She did not understand English; Saul did not speak German. She saw only that his skin was dark, and she had heard fearsome tales about "redskins."

When Bill rode through the stone arch on his spotted Appaloosa, Mama drew all the children into the kitchen. She locked the door. Then she ran through the house pulling curtains shut.

Hans began to cry. "What's wrong, Mama?" he blubbered.

Otto knew what was wrong. Mama was afraid; afraid of space, of mountains and river, afraid of loneliness, afraid of the unknown. Since Otto, too, felt insecure without Bill, he did not know how to help her. He could only say helplessly, "Look, Mama . . ."

Katherine took charge. Briskly she said, "We can't sit around here all day. We must go to school, and so must you, Mama. This is Monday, you know. Now! What shall we pack in our lunches?"

Mama fluttered her hands. A little awkward with embarrassment, she walked back through the house. She opened the curtains.

Food she knew. A lunch she could plan. She decided, "We'll put our food in one basket. We will picnic. Gussie, bring the eggs; Martin, the cupcakes from the pantry; Otto, the milk——"

"Yes, Mama!" each boy answered and rushed off to

127

perform his task while Mama brushed and braided Katherine's long, blond hair.

Otto and Gussie led the horses to the edge of the porch. Otto put Gussie behind his saddle. Hans shared the saddle itself. Martin and Katherine rode together. The third horse was for Mama. Bill had used a blanket skirt to train it for her use.

Mama handed Otto the lunch basket and stepped back. "Today I'll be busy," she said. "Some other day."

"Mama?" Katherine chided. "You promised Bill."

Mama backed toward the kitchen door.

Otto whistled shrilly through his fingers. Saul Whiteclaw started from barn to house. Otto told Mama, "Saul will put your horse back in the corral after we're gone."

Mama cast one glance at Saul. Hastily she scrambled up onto the gentle mare. Otto swallowed a lump of sympathy. Poor Mama; afraid to go to school, afraid to stay home with Saul.

At school Mrs. Pringle set Mama to learning her ABC's. Mama paid scant attention till she discovered Hans was learning the letters faster than she. She set to work.

Mrs. Pringle instructed Otto, "Tell her she's to recite the alphabet from A to Z and point out the letters when I write them on the board. This is her assignment for Friday."

Otto explained carefully. Mama surprised him. She responded to Mrs. Pringle with two words in English, the first he had ever heard come from her lips. "Anna . . . know."

By Friday Mama did know her ABC's, and so did Hans, who was not old enough to go to school, but was there because he could not be left at home. Mama glowed with pride in herself and son. The whole family played a touch-and-name game with Mama. "Table," they said. "Chair. Horse. Sky. Plate. Food." Mama clapped her hands with glee when she managed to say the word before Hans.

On Mama's second Monday at school they found a letter in the crossroads mailbox. It was from Bill, the first mail they had received since coming to Idaho.

"Read," Mama said in English. She pushed the letter into Katherine's hands.

With their three horses crowded shoulder to shoulder, the whole family listened eagerly while Katherine read the words, written in German for Mama's benefit.

Dear Anna, I am happy to tell you I have found work in the Sunshine mine up here in the Coeur d'Alenes. I live at the company's boarding house. All my expenses are held out of my check. I won't be paid for a month, but when I get it, I will send my whole check. Tell Otto I don't mind working underground after all. Regards, your husband, Bill Check.

Mama's eyes brightened, then darkened. She asked anxiously, "Does Bela mind working in the mine?"

"Sure," Hans answered wisely. "Papa likes the sky and the river."

"Is that true, Otto?" Mama asked.

"Yes, Mama," Otto told her. "You remember his scar? He was hurt in a mine a long time ago."

"And *I* made him go back?" Mama asked. She turned to

129

Katherine. "Put the letter in your pocket. We will hurry home to answer it. You will leave it in the mailbox tomorrow as you go to school."

That night Otto sat at the table to write to Bill. Once he had sat at another table in another place to write to this man. Otto's fingers trembled, remembering.

In English Mama said, slowly and soberly, "Tell . . . Bela . . . Anna . . . learn."

"I'll tell him all of us are learning, Mama," Otto said.

Otto, Martin and Gussie enjoyed working with Saul Whiteclaw. Katherine teased, "If Saul told you to saddle your horse backward, you'd try." But she smiled. She, too, liked the young Indian, whose books were propped against bales of hay and in mangers. Since the children missed Bill, they talked to Saul.

Speaking for the whole family, Gussie confessed, "I get kinda mixed up, talking to Mama."

"Your mama is trying to keep her promise," Saul told Gussie. "That is important."

"I guess so," Gussie said, unconvinced. "I wish I knew what she says."

Mama's English sounded like no language any of the Meyers had ever heard, even in the slums of Pittsburgh.

The winter months in the Salmon river country were mild compared to the weather Otto had known in Pittsburgh. Still, it took courage to ride the miles to and from school. Early and late the children took care of the animals.

Not one of the Meyers realized that Christmas was coming till they received Bill's first pay check. He wrote, "All I earn is for you and the kids, Anna. Perhaps you can ride to Whitebird for Christmas treats."

Christmas! Otto remembered carols and lighted candles and Pastor Schmidt's gentle voice reading the Christmas story: "And it came to pass in those days . . ."

Here in Bill's hidden valley, behind the great stone arch, it was easy to picture the shepherds "keeping watch over their flocks by night." Saul Whiteclaw slept in a snug room in the barn loft. He guarded the livestock at night. In Pittsburgh the smoke from steel mills had covered the stars. Here they hung like lanterns from a silvered ceiling. In this land Christmas could "come to pass."

"Will we buy presents?" Hans wanted to know.

Thriftily Mama folded Bill's check and put it in her pocket. She forgot to speak English when she answered. "I gave away Bela's money. I must replace it. Since I cannot earn, I can only save the money he sends me."

Wisely, Katherine said, "Mama, Bill doesn't want to be paid back. He wants us to be happy. If he were here, he would buy Christmas presents for everybody. Remember last Christmas? He sent presents and didn't even sign his name."

"Otto?" Mama questioned.

"It's up to you, Mama," Otto reminded. "Bill says you are head of the Check family while he's away."

"Then I think we will go to Whitebird," Mama said. When she patted her pocket, her face looked young. Otto noticed she did not pat the pocket that held the check. She patted Bill's folded letter.

The long ride to Whitebird was not a spur-of-the-moment trip. They talked about it for days, whispered behind hands, giggled over Christmas secrets and caught up on their work in the corral and barn. At last Saul hitched the workhorses to the wagon and drove through the stone arch. Neither Otto nor Mama had learned to manage a team.

Before they shopped for themselves, they mailed a Christmas box to Bill. Mama had knitted thick gray socks. Katherine baked cookies. Otto and Martin pulled taffy. Martin added a note, "We washed our hands. We don't know why the candy turned gray." Gussie wrote a Christmas verse. Hans had kept his red lead pencil, his farewell present from Tom-the-printer. Hans used it to draw a fancy border around Gussie's verse.

Mama and the children spent Saturday night with Bill's friends, the Wilsons. There Mama spoke haltingly in English.

Mrs. Wilson said heartily, "Bless you, honey! I had you figgered out all wrong. You're gonna do all right in this here valley."

Otto glowed with pleasure.

For the first time in many months, the family went to church. Otto and Katherine listened with close attention in order to tell Mama about the sermon. They knew each time she heard a familiar word, for she bobbed her head till the scarf slid from her blond braids. Mama's lips moved while she repeated words. Once Katherine whispered loudly behind her hands, "Ssh, Mama. We're not supposed to talk out loud."

"Ach, this English," Mama whispered back.

Before they left the village Sunday morning, the sheriff leaned against a front wagon wheel. He reported, "Can't seem to catch up with that peddler feller. He must be holed up back in the sticks. Come spring, he'll have to come out for grub. Then we'll nab him."

When Saul turned towards the bridge, Mama looked back at the sheriff. She asked Otto, "Does *he* speak English?"

Otto grinned and repeated Mama's question to Saul. The Indian laughed aloud. "Ma'am, that's what we call it in the West," he told Mama.

Hours later, when they drove through the stone arch, Otto stood up in the wagon. He grasped Saul's arm. "Look!" he said, pointing into the gathering gloom. "Something is wrong. The horses and cows are in the same corral."

Saul slapped the reins on the backs of the brown horses. When they did not move quickly enough, he flicked their rumps with a whip.

In the corral, west of the big barn, both horses and cows moved in restless circles, making nervous sounds. A barn door stood open. Up at the end of a meadow, a light flickered.

"Somebody is carrying a lantern," Katherine said anxiously.

"Yeah, but where is he going?" Gussie asked. "Nobody lives back there."

"That's right, Saul," Otto said, his voice loud with excitement. "There's nothing back there but mountains at the head of Hell's Canyon."

"Depends on how far you go," Saul answered.

14

The Search

Saul Whiteclaw drove the wagon to the edge of the porch and headed for the barn on the run. The five children ran at his heels. Hans shouted, "Don't catch the man before I get there, Saul!"

"Count the horses, Otto," Saul ordered, "while I search the barn. The rest of you kids keep out till I'm sure there's no danger."

Saul found nobody in the barn, but Otto reported a missing horse.

"That's what I thought was up," Saul said. "Now, who would want a horse, and why?"

"To ride," Hans said wisely.

"I shouldn't have gone to Whitebird," Saul said worriedly. "Otto, take the kids back to the house and help your mother unload the wagon. It's pretty dark, but I may be able to figure out where our visitor is going."

Mama met the children at the edge of the porch. She reported shrilly, "A window is broken, and the house, ach, you should see it. Upside down!"

"Is anything missing?" Katherine asked.

"Is anyone in the house?" Otto asked soberly.

Mama clutched the scarf at her throat. "I didn't think of that, Otto," she gasped. "Will you . . ." Suddenly Mama stood straight. She ordered, "Stay outside. I will do my own searching."

Though comfortable, the house was not large. Soon Mama returned. "Come in, come in," she urged. "We must build fires and clean up this mess."

When fires crackled in range and heaters and heavy coats were removed, a room-by-room search was made. Several things were missing: a thick wool blanket from Otto's bed; a jacket Bill had left hanging on a wall peg in the hall; flour, sugar coffee, two hams and a sack of potatoes.

"We're feeding somebody," Otto said angrily. Helplessly he clenched his fists. He said gruffly, "Come on, Gussie. We must take care of the horses."

The patient brown horses had stood at the edge of the porch. The minute Otto picked up the driving lines, they moved at a brisk trot toward the barn, food, water and warmth. By the time the horses had been rubbed down and fed, the night was black-dark. Gussie helped by carrying a lantern to light Otto's chores.

Big bowls of thick, hot soup waited for Otto, Gussie and Saul. It was almost midnight before Saul had returned. Tiredly he reported, "I went to the head of the valley. It was too dark to tell deer and elk trails from a pack trail. I'll try again, as soon as it gets light."

Mama did not go to school on Monday. "Someone must

stay at the ranch while Saul is away, in case those thieves return," she said.

As the children rode toward the stone arch, Mama shouted in English, "My lesson bring!"

Otto looked back with a feeling of wonder. Could this be Mama? Staying alone in the only ranch house at this end of the valley? Knowing Saul Whiteclaw would be in and out of the house all day? Eager for her next lesson? Speaking a topsy-turvy kind of English?

Saddle leather creaked as Katherine came alongside. She said, "You're smiling, Otto. What are you thinking about?"

"Mama."

"I'm proud of her, too." Katherine needed no explanation.

At the supper table that night, Saul reported. "Someone butchered a calf at the head of the meadow, up where we saw the lantern. It would take a month of Sundays to figure out where he took it. Snow has covered the tracks."

When he could spare time from regular chores, Saul searched the rough country. While they worked together in the barn, he told Otto, "It's slow work."

"I know," Otto agreed. "There's a lot of space out there."

Ed Tippitt had a dollar to spend for Christmas. Otto and Katherine rode with him to Whitebird to spend it. They brought back flour, sugar and coffee to replace stolen supplies.

Mama scolded anxiously, "This is not fair to Bela. Even our food he buys twice!" Her eyes went to the shelf and the can that had held Bill's wallet.

137

Quietly Otto said, "It can't be helped, Mama. When shall I cut our Christmas tree?"

Martin sat by the stove, oiling boots. He looked up eagerly and repeated, "A tree?" That was a luxury the Meyers had never afforded. In Pittsburgh they had made do with looking at the decorated trees in school and church.

In a brief flash of memory, Otto heard Papa ask, "Who wants a Christmas tree?" Papa had wiggled his eyebrows. His children laughed, but not very loudly.

Two days before Christmas the five rode to the top of the hill behind the meadow. Up there a young forest of pines and some firs grew along a creek that ran to the Salmon river. While Otto thumped away with a hatchet, Katherine rode to the crest of the hill. Quickly she rode back down the trail, shouting, "Otto, Martin! I saw smoke in the sky!"

"Is it big smoke? Is our house burning?" Fright showed through Martin's rushing words. Hans' lips began to wobble. Gussie reached for Martin's hand. All eyes turned to Otto.

Katherine shook her head. Her scarf swung in the cold wind. "No, no! There isn't enough smoke for a burning building. It's just —" she finished lamely, "— smoke."

"Martin, help me wrap the Christmas tree with this gunnysack," Otto ordered, "and we'll go see what's burning."

Martin dropped to his knees to help control the branches of the evergreen. While Otto tied the bundle behind his saddle, Martin led patient old Brownie to stand beside a boulder. He scrambled into the saddle, but could not haul

138

up his brothers to share Brownie's broad back. He gasped, "You've got on too many clothes. You're heavy!"

The Meyers were used to "taking care" of Martin. Otto stood beside Brownie. He bowed his back to make a platform for Hans and Gussie to use to mount the horse.

The little group guided their three horses back the way Katherine had come. She stopped when they faced a rock formation that looked like a tumbledown toadstool. She pointed across the valley. There it was: a column of gray smoke in the cold blue sky.

"Is there a house over there?" Katherine asked.

Back in September Otto had ridden the outer fences of the ranch with Bill. He had a reasonably accurate picture of the area in his mind. "No," Otto said. "That could be a campfire. We'd better tell Saul."

Several times Otto stopped his horse, Blaze, to look back at the place where they had seen the smoke. "Should I have gone to investigate?" he fretted. The answer popped into his mind. He could hear Bill Check say firmly, "While I am gone, Anna, you are the head of the family, not Otto."

Before the trail turned, Otto looked back to fix the picture in his mind. Because he knew it was there, he could see the gray thread in the sky. Down at the ranchhouse, Saul might not have noticed, so quickly had the wind thinned and spread the smoke.

Otto nudged his horse's ribs. He shouted, "Move out!"

At the head of the meadow, the horses quickened their pace. They headed for the warm barn. Otto had to struggle with Blaze to make him go to the house.

Mama saw Otto ride up the avenue of leafless young fruit

trees. With her arms wrapped in her big apron, she waited
on the porch. She called, "Ach, such laziness. You could
have carried that tree, Otto. Feet you forget you have.
Horses, always horses, it is!"

Otto slid to the porch and began to untie the Christmas
tree. "Where's Saul?"

"Have we trouble?" Mama asked anxiously.

"Maybe not," Otto said. He heaved the Christmas tree
to the porch floor. "We saw smoke."

"Smoke, ach—" Mama's hands erased the statement from
the air.

"This isn't Pittsburgh, Mama," Otto said patiently.
"Where there's smoke, there's fire, and . . ."

Mama's blue eyes blazed with sudden comprehension.
"And where there's fire, somebody cooks the food stolen
from Bela Czek?"

"Right."

"I'll dress," she snapped. "Saddle my horse."

"But, Mama . . ."

"Saddle!"

While Mama put on warm clothing, she shouted the
news that Saul had ridden to the crossroads mailbox.

Glad for the chance to make a sensible plan, Otto said,
"We'll wait for him."

"We go," Mama said. "Now!"

"But . . ."

"No buts."

Otto saddled Mama's own horse and led it to the porch.
Pelting Otto with questions he could not answer, Gussie,
Martin, Hans and Katherine followed him from the barn.

141

When Mama came onto the porch she wore Bill's oldest coat and her own big shawl. The children stood in an openmouthed row. Crisply Mama said, "Flies you will catch."

Obediently the four shut their mouths. Mama ordered, "In the house, stay." Four heads nodded.

Mama was so determined, she did not even look back to see if Otto followed. She rode toward the skyline.

"Be careful!" Katherine called in a quavering voice.

Otto raised his hand. He followed Mama, helplessly aware that they were on a fool's journey, but knowing he could not let Mama go alone.

Hooves rang on stones protruding from frozen earth. Leather squeaked. Horses blew through nostrils. Wind burned faces. Otto scarcely noticed. He was puzzled by the drapery of Mama's shawl. The left side hung in body-covering softness. Near her right hand there was an oddly stiff fold. No matter which way her body bent, that fold did not change. What was Mama carrying?

On a climbing trail-curve, Otto's temper flamed. Mama's purse was hanging from the pommel of her saddle!

Didn't Mama have a lick of sense? She had wasted Bill Check's ranch profit when she traded with the peddler. Was she going to throw away his mine wages, too? Did Mama think she could bargain with a *thief?*

Angrily, Otto tried to reason with Mama. "Your purse, Mama—"

"Shush," Mama said sharply. "Thinking, I am."

"We're getting close to the rock," Otto pleaded. "Don't you think we should make a plan?" No question about it,

Otto knew they should make a plan. If Mama had a lick of brains in her head, she should know it, too. Otto urged, "I could sneak around and see where he staked out Bill's horse."

"Ja, ja," Mama agreed, but Otto was sure she did not grasp what he said. Against the folds of her big shawl, Mama's jaw looked as solid and unyielding as the toadstool rock that loomed ahead. If Bill could see Mama now, he would not call her a child-woman.

But there was that purse! Had Mama ever acted so foolishly? "Mama . . ." Otto began.

Mama and Otto had no time to plan. The peddler had seen them coming. He stepped out into the trail. His broken teeth showed when he grabbed the reins of Mama's horse. He grinned up into her face.

"Well, if it ain't Missus Check! Howdy. Ya need any pretties today?"

Otto cast a desperate glance at Mama, begging with his eyes that she take care.

Only seconds earlier Mama had been a woman carved from stone. Suddenly she cringed, cried and twittered. Her hands fluttered toward her purse, then jumped into the air and clutched her ears. In English she shrieked, "Take, take!"

The peddler reached for Mama's purse. He said with ugly politeness, "Now, I'd say that's right smart of you."

"No, Mama, no!" Otto begged.

Mama cried and cowered again, but her German words did not match her actions. To Otto's amazement he heard, "Son, if moves the man, the horse stand up!"

143

The Search

Mama moaned again. She reached a shaking, uncertain left hand toward the purse, as if to snatch it from the peddler. Her right arm moved steathily under her big shawl.

With a whoop, the peddler bent his head to explore the purse.

Tensely sitting astride Blaze, Otto looked down into the purse. Empty!

Angrily the peddler lifted his head. He yelled, "You . . . !"

Mama was too quick for the man. She lashed down strongly with the long iron stove poker she had hidden under her shawl. The peddler crumbled in a heap in the snow.

Mama slid from her skirt-trained horse. She looked at the man. Then she uncoiled the rope a western rider always carries. Clumsily but thoroughly she bound the man's hands and feet.

Once the man groaned and moved. Mama ordered, "The horse stand up."

Obediently Otto reared his horse. He had only to command and the hooves would slash like weapons. Otto was glad the man collapsed again.

When Mama was sure the peddler was helpless, she told Otto, "Find Bela's horse."

Poker in hand, Mama stood guard while Otto rode around the toadstool rock and into the man's camp. At first Otto did not see the stolen horse. Then Blaze snickered, and a horse answered. Otto followed the sound and found Bill's horse tethered in a lean-to of pineboughs.

Quickly, Otto untied the stolen horse and led it back to the place where Mama waited. Relief shone in Mama's round face when she saw that the horse was unharmed. She handed Otto her poker. She commanded, "Guard. Bela's coat I must find."

"And my blanket!" Otto reminded.

When Mama returned from the crude camp, she carried the jacket, blanket and one uncut ham. She looked grimly triumphant, but angry, too. She said, "The money I did not find. Now we go."

Together Mama and Otto heaved the peddler onto the back of the horse he had stolen. Even after he began to regain consciousness, the man hung there like a bag of meal that sags in the middle.

Slowly the odd procession edged toward home. At the head of the meadow they were met by Saul Whiteclaw. Angrily he yelled, "What is the meaning of this? You could have gotten yourselves killed if you had met up with that thief! When I report . . ."

Mama's horse and Saul's met on the trail, nose to nose. The angry young Indian saw the man tied on the horse behind Mama. Otto rode as rear guard.

"Flies you will catch," Mama said, with the first glint of humor she had ever displayed toward Saul Whiteclaw.

Saul gulped. He pointed. "Who . . . ?"

"The thief, we found," Mama declared. "Dead we are not. Now, to the sheriff you will take."

"Sure. Yes, ma'am!" Saul said. His voice was respectful. A smile of approval brightened his black eyes.

15

Happy New Year!

When Mama, Saul Whiteclaw, the prisoner and Otto reached the barn, Saul lifted the peddler from the stolen horse. He asked Mama, "What'll I do with this guy?"

"To town we go," Mama snapped.

"In that case, we'll take the wagon," Saul decided. "Draped over a horse, this polecat would freeze. He doesn't deserve it, but we'd better cover him with a horse blanket."

Inside the barn Otto made a blanket pallet for the prisoner. The man did not struggle when Saul dumped him into the wagon bed. This worried Otto. Anxiously, he asked, "Did Mama hit him too hard?"

Saul straightened from having made the man comfortable.

Weakly the prisoner answered for Saul, "I cain't figger out that female."

With a gasp of relief, Otto asked, "What do you mean, figure out?"

"She looks so helpless," the man said, "but she's got the kick of a mule."

147

Mama looked both pleased and embarrassed. Saul grinned.

While Saul set about harnessing the browns, Otto took care of the three riding horses. Once the prisoner twisted his head. Mama brandished her poker. The man lay back and shut his eyes.

Saul helped Mama to the wagon seat. He took his own place at her left and picked up the reins.

"Move out!" Mama ordered. The words were English, but Mama's accent was strange. Saul chuckled aloud as he bounced the lines on the team's broad backs.

Otto closed and fastened the barn door, then ran behind the wagon. He caught up when Saul stopped at the edge of the porch.

Katherine opened the kitchen door. She shouted, "We stayed, Mama, just as you said. Please, may we come out? What's going on?" She stepped out, followed by the three younger boys.

Mama pursed her lips. She gave Katherine's question some thought. Then she said, "To Whitebird, we go, all."

"Who'll take care of the horses?" softhearted Gussie asked in a small voice.

"An' the cows," Hans added.

Martin rolled his eyes toward the barn. He reminded, "Remember what happened last time we went to White-bird?"

"Better than last time will be this," Mama said crisply. "The thief we got."

148

Otto noticed that Saul watched Mama as she had once watched him. Ready to accept any changes Mama might suggest, Saul planned, "Ed Tippitt will lend a hand. We'll see him on our way to Whitebird. Have you kids had your supper? Better grab something for a snack, and dress warmly. We have miles to cover."

After the brief stop at the Tippitt ranch, Mama, Saul and the five children drove all that cold night to deliver the peddler to the sheriff.

At Whitebird the sheriff shared his morning coffee with the cold travelers. He listened to Mama's story of the capture. With a blank face he appealed to Saul. "What did she say?"

With great dignity, Mama told him, "In English I told. English I speak now, always."

The sheriff wiped his forehead. He breathed, "Yeah?"

Saul smiled, but Otto thought Saul looked proud of Mama. Saul stayed with the sheriff while he booked the peddler. Mama and the children called on Mrs. Wilson.

Bill's friend shouted gladly, "If I ain't glad to see ya! How're ya makin' out?" With noisy good humor she welcomed the family into a kitchen that smelled of pumpkin pie and roast beef. By the time Mama's story was told again, the sheriff came with Saul to report. He rolled his hat in big hands and grinned at Mama.

"Seems like that peddler feller had a run of bad luck, meetin' up with you, Mrs. Check. First place, he couldn't spend all of those hundred-dollar bills without folks catchin' onto the fact that he was the thief we wanted. Winter closed in. He couldn't get out of the district without spending Bill's money. He was kinda between the Nez Perces an' the Blackfeet, you might say." Hastily the sheriff turned to Saul Whiteclaw. "No offense, Saul."

"I agree with you. He was between the devil and the deep blue sea." Saul spoke gravely, but his black eyes warmed with amusement.

"Yeah," the sheriff agreed. "Exactly. Figgerin' that he had to eat till spring, the thief moved in on you folks and helped himself to vittles and a horse—"

"What's vittles?" Hans interrupted.

"Ssh," Katherine whispered behind her hands. "He means food."

"Why didn't he say so?" Hans asked loudly. Otto poked Hans' ankle with his foot. Hans was more interested in the sheriff than in a mere brother. He simply moved his foot.

The sheriff went on, "The feller didn't figger on runnin' up against a right smart woman. After all, he had cheated her once, he thought he could do it again. Now, how's this for a Christmas present?" The sheriff laid Bill's wallet in Mama's hands.

"W—why w—where . . . ?" Otto and Mama stammered. Mama's hands shook so much she dropped the wallet on Mrs. Wilson's floor. Hastily Mama picked up the purse. With both hands she hugged it under her chin. Her round pink face glowed with joyous relief.

The sheriff glowed right back at Mama. He said, "We like

old Bill. I'm glad we're able to give back what is rightfully his."

"We searched," Otto said wonderingly.

"Not deep enough," the sheriff said, grinning. "He had Bill's wallet stashed away inside his 'long johns.'"

It took some time to make Mama understand that the sheriff referred to the peddler's heavy woolen underwear.

In the laughter that followed, Mrs. Wilson said, "We've gotta let Bill know he can come home."

A candle lighted behind Mama's blue eyes, then flickered out. She quavered, "So far, he is."

"We'll send a telegram," Mrs. Wilson explained.

Mama knew nothing of telegrams, nor did any of her five children. The whole group went into the heart of the village to send the message to Bill's boardinghouse at the Sunshine Mine. Saul and Mrs. Wilson wrote words on paper, counted words, crossed out words and wrote again till they had exactly ten words. A crowd gathered at the switchboard. Otto remembered the people who had watched while he bought railroad tickets. They had laughed.

These people laughed, too, but Otto liked the sound of their voices. These people said, "Good work, sheriff!" "Hear Bill Check got his money back. Couldn't happen to a nicer guy." "So this is the Check family. Glad to meet you!"

Mama held out one of the hundred-dollar bills to pay for the telegram. The sheriff raised a hand, palm out, as if to ward off further trouble about the money. "Keep your

151

change, Mrs. Check. This telegram is on the house."

Mama's lashes flew upward. Hans' mouth opened to question.

Otto said, in German for Mama's instant understanding, "It's a gift."

With tears in her blue eyes, Mama murmured, *"Gott sei dank."* She wiped her eyes, blew her nose, then said firmly in her own kind of English, "Glad, I am. Thanks I give you." Severely she frowned at Otto. "Why the English you do not say when to school you go?" Mama made shushing motions, moving her children toward the door, the street and the wagon. Shaking his head with wonder at this new Mama, Otto was last to reach the wagon.

Hunching in the cold wind and hugging herself, Mrs. Wilson said, "This is Christmas Eve. Won't you spend it with us? You're more than welcome, honey!"

Mama whispered, *"Weihnachts abend."*

Martin said wistfully, "We have a tree."

"Our first tree,' Katherine explained.

"Otto chopped it," Gussie said proudly.

Hans was never at a loss for words. He reminded Gussie, "Before Trinka saw the smoke."

Though Mama and the children spoke to Mrs. Wilson and the sheriff, they found they were talking to each other, too. Mama raised her chin. Soberly and gladly she said, "We go home."

Again the family and Saul drove all night, but without the prisoner in the wagon bed. Huddled under horse blankets, they sang Christmas carols. As they had done on hot evenings in Pittsburgh, they shared their fund of stories. When they ran out of remembered stories, Hans said sleepily, "Tell about the stranger's mountain."

"Silly, we live there!" Gussie reminded. He poked Hans' sturdy back.

"Oh, yes," Hans said and promptly fell asleep.

Otto thought of all that had happened since the tall stranger had knocked on the door while Martin was in Dr. Wong's hospital. Otto was glad it was dark. He did not have to explain the tears that dampened his eyelashes.

Ed Tippitt had taken good care of animals and buildings. The house was warm and breakfast coffee bubbled on the wood-burning stove. In the middle of the coming-home excitement, he shouted, "Christmas gift!"

"What is this Christmas gift?" Mama asked in amazement.

Mischievously Ed said, "It means I get to open the first present from the Christmas tree."

Katherine squealed, "Christmas tree! It's out on the porch!" She rushed through the door and onto the back porch. There she shrieked, "It's gone! Our tree is gone!"

"Just like last time," Martin said unhappily. "Robbers."

Loose-jointed as a colt, Ed Tippitt crossed the kitchen and opened the door into the large living room. He shouted, "Merry Christmas!"

Open-mouthed, Mama, Otto, Katherine, Martin, Gussie and Hans moved toward the decorated Christmas tree that stood in the corner, where wide windows looked out on mountains, valley and river. Saul blew his nose loudly when the little family joined hands and tiptoed around the tree, strung with popcorn, cranberries and the paper rings pasted at school. The family's presents hung from branches or lay under the boughs.

With shining eyes Katherine told Ed, "Thank you. We've never had a tree. It's beautiful."

Ed squirmed and blushed. "Aw . . ." He scrubbed the shining floor with one boot toe. "It was Christmas Eve, and I kinda celebrated." He turned to Mama. "I hope you don't mind, ma'am, but my folks came over to keep me company. Mom helped me fix up the tree. She found where you hid the presents, and she put them under the tree."

"Ja, ja," Mama said. She bobbed her head while she watched the words come out of Ed's mouth.

"Well, where's Ed's present?" Hans asked loudly.

"Choose!" Katherine urged.

Blushing, but grinning, Ed chose a small package that dangled from a bough. When he tore off the tissue paper, Ed held up a bar of pink, perfumed soap.

Mama protested, "Again you take! For Katrinka, that is."

Pocketing the pink soap, Ed said, "I like this fine. Just fine." It was Katherine's turn to blush.

"Presents?" Gussie begged.

Saul ordered cheerfully, "Wait for me! I must take care of the horses."

"I'll help," Ed offered quickly.

"So will I!" Otto said, glad for the chance to step out

into the cold morning. While he worked his emotions quit jumping like a monkey on a string.

After breakfast Ed stayed long enough to watch Katherine open a tiny package wrapped in red tissue paper and stuck in a brown pine cone. She gasped with pleasure when she found a locket made of a perfect Indian arrowhead and a length of velvet ribbon. She whispered, "Thank you, Ed."

"Aw . . ." Ed mumbled, then hastily took his leave. The whole family stood on the porch to wave and shout, "Merry Christmas!" till the long-legged boy rode his Appaloosa through the great stone arch.

Christmas was good, but New Year's Eve was better. At exactly midnight Mama, the children and Saul stepped out onto the porch to raise a clatter with pot lids, wooden spoons, cowbells and a willow whistle Hans had saved from summer. They shouted, "Happy New Year!" each to the other, and listened to the echo that bounced from the mountainside behind the arch.

But one answer was not an echo.

A glad "Halloo!" rang like a bell in the cold night. The children stopped their noisemaking to listen. Mama put trembling fingertips over her mouth. She whispered, "Can it be?"

"Happy New Year!"

"Bela Karl!" Mama called in a glad, trembling voice.

"Papa!" shouted Otto, Katherine, Martin, Gussie and Hans.

155

Such a homecoming! Arms opened wide. Hearts spoke of happiness through smiling lips. Eager hands fumbled for Bill's coat buttons and heavy scarf. Otto rode to the barn on Bill's spotted Appaloosa. Gussie overcame his fear of dark and lonely places and rushed to help Otto take care of Bill's horse. In the barn the horse flicked his ears, exploring this familiar space, and made little talking sounds of gladness. Gussie declared happily, "He's glad to be home."

Together Otto and Gussie raced back to the house lest they miss one word of family talk.

Mama poured coffee and milk and cut a huge apple pie. In English she begged, "Is good, I baked. Eat, eat!"

"Anna," Bill said quietly. "You're not speaking German."

Mama's chin raised. "Is it in Germany I am? Always this English I speak now."

Bill reached for one of Mama's work-reddened hands. He kissed the finger that wore his gold ring. He said, "I'm proud of you, Anna."

Mama ducked her head. Blond lashes covered her blue eyes, but her hand snuggled deeper into Bill's big palm.

While they ate and laughed, asked and answered questions, the story was retold of Mama's capture of the thieving peddler.

Seeing the respect in Bill's gray eyes, and the color in Mama's round cheeks, Otto realized that the real story was in their hearts. Bill had believed in Mama, and Mama had responded when given the freedom to "grow up." While Mama gained confidence, her children grew with her,

mentally and physically, and fitted themselves into a new life. Even Bill had grown. Otto sensed that Bill had overcome his fear of mine tunnels. Bill no longer rubbed the scar in its little circle of white hairs. In this room, each person was free to speak and to act.

"Freedom," Otto thought. "Papa's ladder."

For the briefest of moments, Otto seemed to see and hear Papa, sitting in his rocking chair, and talking about his ladder that reached from "here to there." Somehow, in Otto's remembering, Papa's "there" became Bill Check's "here," for Mama was leading Bill to Papa's chair and telling him, "Your eyes shut. I come."

Briefly Mama left the room. When she came back her apron pocket bulged with something she had hidden there. She carried Gussie's slate and chalk. She said, "Bela Karl, your eyes open." Mama placed the wallet in Bill's hand.

Obediently Bill opened his eyes. He did not open the purse or count the money. He simply held the wallet. His face went red, then white, then red again while Mama balanced the slate on one of his knees. The chalk squeaked while she printed, slowly and carefully, "V luv U."

Bill hesitated, then slowly picked up the slate. His lips moved, but no sound came out.

Katherine said softly, "Doesn't Mama write well, Papa? Shall I read it for you?"

Bill nodded at Katherine, but kept his eyes on Mama's face.

"We love you," Katherine read softly.

Bill stood up. He said, "And I love you."

158

Bill's eyes and voice included each child: Otto, Katherine, Martin, Gussie, Hans and even Saul Whiteclaw, but his arms went around Mama.

"That's the way it should be," Otto thought. "He's the man of the family."

"Happy New Year," Hans muttered sleepily. Suddenly his blue eyes opened doll-wide. He slid from his chair and headed for the door to the porch.

"Hansel, you go where?" Mama demanded.

"I lost my willow whistle," Hans said. He peered into the dark. Holding the heavy door ajar, his eyes invited Otto to follow.

Otto grinned. In broad daylight Hans might be a "native son," but in the dark he was still the youngest Check in need of a big brother's help.

"I'll help you find your whistle, Hans," Otto offered. "Wait till I light a lantern."